AF492602

THE MYSTIC

and other stories for seekers

DANIEL M^cKENZIE

Going Down

The applause was thunderous, like stock tickers hitting all-time highs.

Derek Lang smiled, palms open as if accepting a divine offering, then clapped once—at himself. The stage lights warmed his face, haloing his perfectly tousled hair. Behind him, a massive LED screen read: "THE ALGORITHM OF WINNING: HACKING LIFE ON YOUR TERMS."

"Remember," he said, pacing with the confidence of a prophet, "the universe doesn't reward the humble—it rewards the hungry. Play nice if you want to lose," he said. "Or play smart if you want to win."

Laughter, mostly from men in tailored blazers and crypto-logo pins. Phones were out, already capturing soundbites for social media. Somewhere in the back, a VC with teeth like bleached piano keys shouted, "Hell yeah!"

He grinned. "Look, I didn't grow up rich. I just refused to stay poor. Life's a game. I figured out the code. Code your own future, or get coded by someone else. Simple."

He paused for effect, letting the silence inflate his ego one last time.

"Time," he said, glancing at his Rolex, "is the only real currency. And I'm buying it in bulk."

More applause. Standing ovation. Derek gave a mock bow and exited stage left, already fishing his phone out of his jacket.

His assistant trotted beside him, whispering updates. "Your jet's wheels-up in forty-five. Car's waiting. Next event's in Austin."

"Perfect," Derek muttered, half-listening as he texted something about a yacht party in Ibiza.

Then: buzz. A notification. Flight delay. Severe weather. Airport lockdown.

He frowned. "No. No, no, no."

"Sorry, sir," said the assistant, scanning her phone. "It's grounded. Might be a few hours."

Derek stopped mid-stride, staring at the elevator ahead of him.

"Fine," he snapped. "Let's just get down and out of this circus."

The assistant started to follow but peeled off as her phone rang.

Derek stepped into the elevator alone, muttering under his breath.

Just before the doors slid shut, a short, brown-skinned woman in a housekeeping uniform and cart slipped in. A young girl accompanied her with a half-eaten granola bar in one hand and her mother's worn leather bag in the other.

He barely glanced at them. Background NPCs—that's how he thought of people like them. The kind of looped characters you breeze past in a video game. Necessary for atmosphere. Invisible in practice.

The girl looked up at him, curious.

Derek didn't look down.

The elevator jolted, then stopped between floors shortly after the doors closed.

Silence.

The hum of the building seemed to hold its breath.

Derek glanced at the floor indicator. It blinked. Then froze. He jabbed the "Lobby" button. Nothing. Pressed "Door Open." Nothing. Then, finally: a sigh, and stillness.

"What the f—. You've got to be kidding me," he muttered.

He tapped his phone. No signal, of course. Thirty-two billion dollars in crypto assets, and he couldn't get a single bar inside a glass-and-steel tomb.

The woman beside him shifted her bag quietly. The movement rustled the air, drawing Derek's attention for the first time. She was short—barely to his elbows—but heavy and sturdy, with calm eyes and a uniform embroidered with a tag that read "Carla." Her hair was tied up in a bun using a ball point pen, and her shoes were worn thin at the heels.

Beside her, the girl stood upright and alert. Her black eyes studied him—not with awe or anxiety, but something else. Composure. Something unsettling in someone so young.

Derek cleared his throat and cracked his neck, hoping for a satisfying pop. None came.

"How long's this gonna take?" he asked no one in particular.

The girl turned to her mother, who said something soft in Spanish.

"She says she doesn't know," the girl translated. Her voice was clear and unhurried.

Derek nodded once. "Right. Well, I've got a plane to catch."

Another pause.

The girl turned to her mother again. Another soft exchange.

"She says, the sky will wait," the girl said.

Derek raised an eyebrow. "Very poetic," he said, voice tinged with sarcasm, checking his phone again for any bars.

The girl only smiled.

Derek hadn't always been rich. He liked to say that on stage, though it had been a long time since the phrase carried any real truth. The hunger was gone, replaced by something else: momentum, maybe inertia. The sense that he was no longer climbing, just orbiting.

The real Derek Lang had died somewhere in a WeWork conference room in 2015, after closing his first Series A and being called a "visionary." From that point on, he learned to perform himself—a curated persona of brute optimism, crypto swagger, and just enough cynicism to seem clever.

He knew how to play it humble in interviews. "Oh, I've been lucky," he'd say with a grin. But he didn't believe in luck. Not really. He believed in leverage, in volume. In taking risks bigger than anyone else was willing to. He'd built a digital casino and rigged it so the house always won—and he was the house.

And now?

Now he was stuck in an elevator with a hotel maid and her daughter. No signal. No assistant. No exit. Just a weirdly calm child watching him like she could see beneath his skin.

The girl turned to her mother, who said something else in Spanish. The two of them spoke back and forth—fluid, calm, as if nothing were wrong.

Derek crossed his arms and tapped his foot.

"All right," he said, trying to sound amused. "What's the gossip?"

The girl looked up, "She didn't like your talk."

Derek blinked. "Excuse me?"

"She said… it was full of empty gold."

He frowned. "Empty gold?…She doesn't even speak English."

"She knows enough," the girl said, without malice.

Carla looked at him directly now. Her face calm. Still. She didn't need to understand his words—she had heard his tone.

She said something else, her voice low and steady.

The girl listened, then translated. "She says… no one stands alone. Not even the tallest man."

Derek rolled his eyes. "Look, I didn't come here for a philosophy lesson. I just want to get out of this damn elevator."

More Spanish. The girl listened, nodded, then translated:

"She says, the universe heard you."

He looked up—half in disbelief, half in irritation. "Okay…And?"

The elevator stayed still.

"She says, sometimes the answer is no."

Derek scoffed, but a drop of sweat slipped down his back.

The girl leaned against the mirrored wall, settling in, while her mother remained still and at ease. Derek, by contrast, fidgeted as if the walls were shrinking around him.

"Look," he muttered. "You don't know me."

The girl didn't respond. Her mother watched quietly, her gaze steady but unreadable.

The woman spoke, soft and low.

Then the elevator dropped—a sudden violent jolt.

Just a foot or two, but enough to send the handrail slamming into his palm and the lights flickering once.

Derek braced himself, breath caught.

When he looked down, he saw them. A column of ants emerging from a crack in the floor's edge, scaling the mirrored wall. Neat, ordered. Purposeful.

He stared. "You've got to be kidding me." He raised his shoe.

"Look at how they climb," the girl said. Calm. Observing.

He hesitated.

The mother murmured again.

"They all believe they're going somewhere new."

Derek lowered his foot slightly.

"They don't know they're just following a scent."

He said nothing.

Then the girl added, "Men aren't so different."

Derek narrowed his eyes. "Are you suggesting I'm…?"

The girl didn't flinch. "Only if you forget you're in line."

He looked again at the trail. One ant slipped, faltered. It flailed for a moment before merging back into the pattern.

"They don't leave a name. Just a groove."

He exhaled through his nose. "This is absurd."

The girl tilted her head. "That's what they say when the ground shifts."

A long pause.

Derek was finally beginning to listen to the words. Then he did something strange—he knelt. Not in surrender. Not in revelation. Just… tired. Like someone realizing how much their body had been doing without any thanks.

He sat.

The ants kept climbing.

The mirrored wall threw back their shapes in fractured repetition. Derek stared at them without blinking. His body folded in on itself, breath evening out.

"She says," the girl added gently, "you've been trying to win a game that can't be won."

Derek said nothing.

"Collecting more," she continued. "But to what end?"

He pressed his thumb into his palm. The skin there was raw. He hadn't noticed until now.

The elevator seemed smaller now—not physically, but in density. As if everything inside it had shifted slightly toward something truer.

Derek looked up. His eyes found Carla's. She hadn't spoken in minutes. She hadn't moved. But it felt like she had spoken every word.

"Why now?" he thought. "Why here?"

The girl looked at him, not unkindly. "Because you stopped moving."

The elevator hummed faintly overhead.

Derek sat still, one leg folded beneath him, the other crooked outward. He watched the ants climb in a slow, unbroken rhythm. The mirrored panel behind them caught their ascent, doubling the movement—an endless procession climbing nowhere.

He ran a hand through his hair.

"How long have they been here?" he asked.

The girl shrugged. "Long enough."

He looked up at her, her small frame leaning against the rail.

"They were here before us," she added.

"And?"

She considered. "They'll be here after."

Carla's voice murmured again. Soft. Unhurried.

The girl translated without glancing away from Derek.

"She says, the line forgets the ones who fall."

He watched an ant tumble sideways. It writhed briefly, then vanished into the seam.

"They walk until they vanish," the girl continued. "But the scent remains."

Derek blinked. "You mean… they follow each other's path."

"It's the only path they know," she answered.

He let that settle, then looked away.

Carla hadn't moved. She might have been listening. She might have been praying. She might have been waiting. Her eyes were closed, her breath quiet.

The girl stepped forward, her voice more like breath now.

"She says… the strong believe the path belongs to them. But the path is not theirs."

"Whose is it then?"

She paused.

"The path belongs to the ground."

That caught him. He looked up.

"What does that mean?"

The girl just tilted her head. "You've been walking like the floor owes you something."

He opened his mouth to argue. Then closed it.

He looked at his hands. The cuff of his shirt was rumpled. The watch sat heavy on his wrist.

"But how?" he murmured.

"You asked to rise," the girl said. "But forgot who lifted."

He rubbed his eyes. His voice dropped to a whisper.

"I didn't mean to…"

"To forget?" she offered.

He nodded.

"She says, forgetting is part of climbing. You climb, so, you forget."

The elevator gave a soft click. Then nothing.

The ants kept climbing.

Derek shifted on the floor, running a hand down his pant leg. The fabric felt unfamiliar. Wrong, somehow—like someone else's skin. He scratched absently at his calf, then his forearm.

The ants were multiplying.

Not just one column anymore. Several. From the baseboard, from a vent, from an unseen seam behind the control panel—they emerged in silent numbers, orderly at first, then less so.

He looked up at the mirrored walls.

There were hundreds of them. Marching in reflections. Inverting.

Splitting. Crossing over each other like tangled thoughts in a sleepless brain.

"Jesus," he muttered.

He slapped his arm. Nothing was there.

The girl and her mother hadn't moved. Carla's eyes were still closed. The girl watched quietly, but she no longer seemed curious—only steady. As if she'd seen this before.

Derek tried to swallow, but his throat was dry.

"They're in my clothes," he said. "I can feel them."

He pulled at his collar. Loosened the top button. Scratched his chest.

"They're crawling on me," he whispered, now frantic. "They're crawling—"

He slapped his ankle. Tore open his cuff. Nothing.

But his body wouldn't believe it.

He stood suddenly, breathing hard. Backed against the mirror.

"Get them off me."

The girl spoke, voice like wind through cracks.

"She says… it's not them."

Derek panted. "What?"

"It's the weight," she said. "It has nowhere else to go."

He looked at her. Her outline swam a little. Or maybe it was the elevator. Or maybe it was his own vision, cracking at the edges.

"I want out!" he hissed.

Another ant crept up the inside of his sleeve. This time he saw it. Or thought he did.

He screamed.

Tore off his jacket. Tossed it to the ground.

Clawed at his shirt, leaving red streaks across his chest.

"They're inside," he cried. "Inside me!"

The girl took one small step back. Not in fear. In reverence. Like she was watching a ritual unfold.

"She says…" the girl whispered, "you're not being punished."

"Then what the hell is this?"

"You're being shown."

Derek fell to his knees, shirt torn, hair wild. Sweat ran in rivers down his temple. His breath came in shallow bursts.

Carla opened her eyes.

Not wide. Just enough to see.

And in that look, there was no judgment. No surprise. Just the quiet acknowledgment of a soul being returned to the fire.

The ants climbed still.

Derek stumbled backward. The elevator was now tilting—or maybe it was just him. The mirrored walls shimmered as if slick with heat. He blinked, hard, but the reflections didn't return to normal. They multiplied.

In every panel, the ants were climbing—not just in lines now, but in swarms. And they had faces. Human faces. Familiar ones. Not exact replicas, but masks made from ambition and smirk.

There was a man in a powdered wig, clutching land deeds like gospel. Another with railroad soot on his collar and hunger in his eyes. A man with a monocle and a diamond cane. Tech bros in hoodies and baseball caps. Bankers with hedge fund logos embroidered on their sleeves. Cold eyes. Hungry teeth.

All of them climbing. All of them stepping over each other. Over and over, the same grin pasted onto every face.

Derek gasped. "What—what is this?"

The girl didn't move.

Her voice was low, as if quoting something old:

"She says… these are your kin."

He staggered forward. "No."

"They lived like gods," the girl said. "Above law. Above land. Above people. Until the earth swallowed them whole."

Derek gripped the railing. His reflection grinned back at him—not his real face, but one of the ants wearing his skin.

"She says," the girl continued, "they built pyramids out of flesh and called it destiny."

The elevator began to creak. The mirrored walls flexed, as if breathing. The ants surged upward, stepping on one another's faces, crushing limbs, laughing as they climbed.

He saw their hands now—manicured, gold-ringed. Grasping. Always grasping. A mass of hunger.

"She says," the girl went on, "they each believed they were the final one. The master of the game. But there is no top. Only more climb. And no end. Only gravity."

One of the ants turned its head. It was Derek.

Hundreds of them were.

Each with a slight variation—different watches, different suits, different smirks—but all unmistakably him.

"No," Derek breathed. "No, no, no—"

One Derek-ant slipped. It flailed, then was trampled underfoot by three others. Another laughed as he climbed over his own face.

Derek pressed himself against the corner of the elevator.

"They're me," he whispered.

"They're what comes before you," said the girl. "And what comes after."

The ants swarmed now—not just on the walls, but through the air, as if reality had a seam and they were spilling through it. Their voices were laughter. Greedy, triumphant, hollow.

"You are nothing but a rung," they chorused. "A rung on a ladder that leads nowhere."

Derek panicked.

The ants were crawling over him now—through his collar, into his ears, behind his eyes. Not biting. Just moving. Crawling. Filling the space where his self once lived.

"Stop," he gasped. "Stop—get off me!"

The girl stood still, untouched, watching him with solemn eyes. Her mother remained calm, as if the air itself had thickened to keep the ants away from them.

The swarm thickened. The walls glistened black with movement.

Derek screamed.

And then—

Ding

The doors slid open.

Sound returned first—footsteps in the hallway, the distant clatter of dishes, the soft drone of conditioned air.

Carla pushed her cart forward. The girl followed, chewing the last of her granola bar. Neither looked back

Derek remained where he was.

The hallway appeared exactly as it had before: patterned carpet, recessed lighting, framed abstract prints meant to offend no one. A man in a blazer walked past while speaking into his phone, his voice bright with urgency. Somewhere, someone laughed.

Derek finally stepped out.

His phone buzzed in his hand. He did not look at it.

Across the corridor, the conference banner still hung above the ballroom entrance.

One of the letters flickered.

Then steadied:

THE ALGORITHM OF WINN NG

THE MYSTIC

The End Is Only the Beginning

I collapse onto the grass with exaggerated cinematic flair. I act out my tragic death by falling to my bare knees showing through the tattered holes of my Toughskins. Then, with both hands still over the imaginary abdominal wound, I topple onto my side.

Kushhhhh! Ooooooooooooooh!

My body violently convulses in a few final, desperate spasms before becoming gloriously moribund. All this unfolded on the freshly mowed battlefield outside my family's suburban home.

The rules of the game were simple: once shot, you had to remain silent and still, lying on the ground until someone on your team released you—that is, gave you life again by ceremoniously kneeling next to you, holding their palms face-down above your head, and reciting the words:

You are free! Rise, oh great warrior!

We had played this game hundreds of times using various projectiles to keep it interesting—sometimes darts, sometimes just the acorns that had fallen from the tall oaks lining the street. Other times, when it was hot outside, the weapon-of-choice was water balloons or "water weenies," as we used to call them—surgical rubber tubing tied at one end with a detachable ballpoint pen top at the other for squirting your opponent from a safe distance. Those with water weenies were ruthless against their enemies, but were also left vulnerable when refilling them at whichever neighbor's garden faucet wasn't currently being used.

Despite the varying modes of weaponry, the rules never changed.

The name of the game was to take out as many of the other team's members as possible so there would be no one to release them from their deep, dark sleep. Each team developed its own strategy. We would work together to distract the other team so that any of our dead could be quickly revived and rejoined.

Simulating my awful, ghoulish end, I lie on the ground with my eyes shut. Normally, I would have one open and one closed, carefully avoiding the wrath of my capturers while pleading for a teammate nearby to release me. However, this time is different. Perhaps it was something I ate or had seen on TV the night before that shifted my consciousness and triggered an experience so profound that it would forever change the direction of my life.

Back then, I had a knack for joking around, often drawing inspiration from popular movies, TV shows, cartoons and magazines. I was a bit of a clown, you could say, always pretending to be some superhero or well-known protagonist—much to my friends' amusement.

When I was in character, which was often, I was totally focused—almost possessed. I could spend hours acting out the role of *The Incredible Hulk*, *The Six Million Dollar Man*, or Caine from the *Kung Fu* series, always looking for supporting actors who would play along in my parody. So, it was natural for me to play out my last standing moment—among the flowering jasmine and bougainvillea—with style.

Lying on the cool grass, I begin to wonder, "How far can I fake my own death?"

I imagine that I really have been shot in the gut and that life-force that sustains me is quickly running out.

I imagine the body losing blood, saturating my clothes and the ground below. The eyes roll back. Heat leaves the body as the heart begins to fail.

But then something happens that I wasn't imagining.

Everything goes dark.

Time seems to stop.

I fall into a kind of strange "hypnosis"—for lack of a better term.

I'm thinking:

Death has really come.

I've taken it too far this time.

This is it.

I'm a goner.

And yet, beneath the fear, there is curiosity:

What exactly is dying?

Consciousness slips away from my body and I am now looking down from above. I can see that the body, in reality, is just an empty vessel.

Next, there is a stillness I have never felt before. There are no other thoughts other than the thought of being a witness to this amazing experience. It is an indescribable peace.

It's like that moment when your neighbor's blaring stereo suddenly stops and for a fraction of a second—before anything else can fill the void—a certain clarity shines through. I am now that clarity and in a state of total bliss.

A holy silence encapsulates me.

And then—

"Get up!" yells my best friend Nick, nudging me with his bare foot.

Suddenly, my buddy, remembering the protocol, kneels next to me with palms over my head, reciting: "You are free! Rise, oh great warrior!"

But I am oblivious to Nick and his help.

"Come on, Vic, we need to get the hell out of here before those dickheads come back!"

Still no movement.

"Get up, doofus!" Nick starts kicking me in the butt when I suddenly snap out of my meditative state and emerge back to life.

I feel as if I had just awakened from a deep slumber. The experience leaves me strangely rested and with an incredible sense of calm and fresh re-entry into the world.

"Let's go, Vic. They're coming…Run!!!"

But instead, I just slowly sit up and look around a bit dumbfounded. Nick runs away as the other team begins to close in.

"Dude, I shot you again! Die sucker! Stay down you pussy!" disparages the other side.

But I just sit there as if I had just had a pleasant nap, indifferent to all the chaos.

Not getting a reaction from me, the enemy moves on, leaving me by myself once again.

I remain seated there for some time, perhaps an hour, long after the rest of the kids decide to go inside for popsicles and a few rounds of Pong.

As I sit, recovering from what just happened, the world around has a clarity I've never noticed before.

Every sense is heightened, every detail vivid beyond belief.

The sharp, sweet scent of the freshly cut lawn fills the air with each emerald blade catching the sunlight.

The warmth of the sun hugs me, not just touching my skin, but sinking deep into my bones—as if I am part of it, as if it is part of me.

Above, the sky stretches into a blue so deep, so endless, that I suddenly realize it is infinity itself.

I have just died to the body, yet I have never felt more alive.

There is no fear.

Nothing to hold onto.

Nothing to resist.

Only this—this perfect moment, in a world more vibrant than I've ever known it.

As a result, I become aware of how the body works and thoughts arise, all without any of my doing. It is as if a veil has been lifted, revealing a truth I had always known but never recognized.

The boundaries dissolve, and for a fleeting, boundless moment, I am the perceiver, the perceiving, and the perceived.

Adjusting

It would be several weeks before the pronounced feeling of bliss began to fade. For days after my experience, I barely left my bedroom. This worried my parents, who sensed I was no longer my normal self. I spoke only when spoken to, moved only when an itch demanded it, and spent long stretches sitting upright with my eyes closed, still resting in the afterglow of what had happened.

Free from the pressures of worldly life, my face took on an appearance of unusual serenity. My friends would come over, but would soon leave due to my seemingly listless response. I didn't want to play frisbee, go to the community swimming pool, or even watch TV. I just wanted to sit, continuing to sip the quiet sweetness from within.

Having taken my temperature and showing no symptoms of being ill, my mother began to get concerned. She carefully inquired, "Victor, honey, you've been acting different lately. Is everything okay with you?" checking to see if my forehead was warm, eyes dilated or palms sweaty.

"I'm fine, Mom. Sorry. Really, I'm fine."

Most parents would have followed up with more questions, curious to know if their child had taken something they shouldn't have, or received something from a stranger. They might have called the parents of the friends to see if their boys were demonstrating similar behavior. As a last resort, they might have taken their child to the family doctor to get a thorough examination.

But the calm emanating from me was contagious. Each time my mom, dad, or sister entered my room, their concerns would be assuaged as they felt a wave of peace flow over them. Sure, my behavior was odd for a goofy and extroverted 14-year-old boy who normally had difficulty focusing, sitting still, and frequently found himself in trouble. But to be with me, as my sister later told me, was to experience a strange and rare comfort.

Of all the family members, my sister was the most supportive. She would come to my room and we would just both sit in silence together. There was never a sense of awkwardness between us that I felt with the others, whose answer to stillness was fidgeting. Later, my sister would begin to ask me questions.

She wanted to know every detail about what happened to me that day, and had her own hypothesis about death, believing that nothing ever dies, that everything in this world is recycled—even that part of us we cannot see. It was our conversations that I missed most after I left home. It was my sister who was accepting of what I had become.

On the other hand, my church-going mom, to make herself feel more comfortable with my sudden shift in temperament, would tell all the family and any of the faithful that I must've had an encounter with Jesus that warm summer day lying on the grass. "What else could explain my son's sudden saint-like behavior?" she would ask. It was then, that she started to read about the lives of famous Christian mystics like Meister Eckhart, St. Catherine of Siena and St. John of the Cross, and warned me about the "dark night of the soul."

As days passed, my old sense of self slowly returned and I began to try to integrate myself more with family and friends. But others noticed something different about me. When I started school again that fall, all my old buddies lamented how I had changed. I was no longer the pestering, restless kid, trying to impress his friends by drawing obscene pictures and passing them around, or giving a quarter to anyone who would lick the tetherball pole in the dead of winter.

I would kick around a ball with some of the other guys just to pass time, but no longer was the life of the party. Most of my friends would eventually abandon me, wondering where the old Vic had gone. My social status plummeted and I could now sometimes be found playing tether ball by myself to pass time, or sitting alone on a bench having lunch when Nick wasn't around to keep me company.

Ironically, it was the same girls I used to tease that I now preferred to share company with. With the girls, I could at least talk about my new passions that now included painting and learning to play the guitar. Ever since the day of my death experience, I had gained a greater appreciation for the arts. I could now experience both with a clarity and delight that was absent before.

My eighth grade teacher was pleasantly surprised to see that I had a more serious side, although, she often found me in a day-dreaming stupor. Other than that, my grades were good and when called on in class, I would always give thoughtful answers.

I also became very curious, began to read a lot, and even enjoyed some writing.

My adolescence quickly passed by. Looking back, it all seems like a dream. Childhood, elementary school, the long summer afternoons in New Hinton—they feel real, yet strangely weightless, as if they belonged to someone else. I sometimes wonder if I had truly lived those events. I remember growing up, but did anything really change?

I was now in the second year of that precarious time in life when every high school teenager aimlessly walks the aisles of the identity marketplace trying on various masks to see which one might fit. Fortunately, I never saw the point of it all. After all, isn't a mask for covering up something? And if so, what is it that everyone is in such a hurry to cover up? In contrast to the other kids, I was trying to remove the mask my parents, teachers and society had put on me, not acquire a better-fitting one.

However, my self-esteem struggled in other ways. I now found it almost impossible to connect with others. To me, high school was a strange state of limbo where young men and women were too clever to remain children, but still too stupid to become responsible grown-ups. I was astonished how most of the students behaved— the fads, the makeup, the fear of missing out, the insane-emphasis on everything sports…the fascination with drawing male genitalia on everything.

Unlike some kids who find themselves friendless due to lack of social skills, I became a "loner" by choice and chose to spend my lunch break in or around the library— far away from the jocks, preppies, stoners, and goths. The other kids thought I was a bit odd and reclusive, but for the most part, ignored me. I never wanted to stand out, and if I had had a choice, would've preferred to never be seen or known. I even asked my mom if I could do home study—a proposal that was immediately shot down.

Only the teachers really knew me. They all thought I was a very sensitive, inquisitive and curious student with profound questions. Depending on the teacher, I was encouraged to go onto college and study either biology, physics, psychology or law. But in spite of my good grades and few, but solid relationships, all through high school there was a longing I couldn't ignore. I never forgot what happened that one summer day in front of my parent's house, when I had witnessed a kind of innate essence.

During lunch time and in my free time, I searched for answers to what I might've experienced. I scoured the library for books that would confirm that others had experienced the same. Along the way, I discovered Heraclitus, Marcus Aurelius, Bento de Spinoza, Ralph Waldo Emerson, and Henry David Thoreau—just to name a few. But my search was mostly fruitless, and I had nobody I could trust to share my experience with who might be able to help me make sense of it.

I was on my own, alone in the wilderness.

I had a compass, but no map.

"A Nice Place to Live"

After that summer—after the event—I began noticing things about New Hinton I had never seen before.

New Hinton is a decent-enough place to live. It has plenty of walking space, clearly marked roads, several schools, parks, shops, restaurants, a community center, an old steeple church, a bustling downtown area full of bookstores, art galleries and antique shops, and several fraternal organizations.

There is also a burger joint and a new car wash that lets you sit in your car while it goes through. The Cineplex always has long ticket lines on the weekends, and the bowling alley and roller skating rink are frequented by fun-seekers. Everyone is very cordial and neighborly, and—well, if this all sounds like something that has been portrayed, ad nauseam, as the ideal American city in dozens of old black and white movies, you would be right.

New Hinton is a cliché. A beloved and revered stereotype. Upon entering the main road going into downtown, there is a nicely painted sign, adorned with an array of petunias and marigolds at its base. It states the obvious:

New Hinton - "A Nice Place to Live."

As such, there's nothing particularly remarkable about New Hinton, except for the fact that everything seems to run like clockwork—including the people who live there. Everyone has a role and they perform it seamlessly, without complaint—from the crosswalk guard to the street cleaner, the baker to the window washer. Even the garbage collector moves through his routine with effortless dance-like precision. I suppose that's not a bad thing. In fact, it's likely the reason New Hinton functions so well.

People come out in the evenings to interact with their neighbors and participate in civic engagement. Businesses and politics prioritize long-term communal well-being, over short-term individual gain. Sure, New Hinton has its cast of characters and challenges, but in general, it lives up to its description.

I once met an old foreigner at the bookstore where I used to work who compared New Hinton to a movie he saw many years ago. When I asked him to describe the plot, he said it was about a man who, unbeknownst to him, grows up on an actual television production set as the star of the show. This poor guy later discovers that his entire life has been scripted and that all the town's people, and even his wife and best friend, are just actors! But I have never seen such a movie at the Cineplex or on television, and doubt that it even exists. And yet, sometimes I sense that, like the story's clueless protagonist, I'm also living on a production set and that nothing is what it seems.

Several people say they've witnessed UFO's and other unexplainable phenomena. One time, at noon on a cloudless day, a darkened and strangely geometric-shaped patch seemed to form in the sky. We all saw it. It seemed to grow in size, its edges flickering with a shimmering glow of red, blue, and green, and then suddenly it dissipated as the actual sky began to fill it in with blocks of blue. Reality itself seemed to be repairing the breach. Oddly, the news never reported it, and everyone just seemed to stop talking about it soon after.

Another time, for several days, there was no night. An entire week passed by without darkness. This, of course, had the effect of throwing off everyone's circadian rhythm so that people were walking around at all hours of the day like zombies, working, shopping and getting chores done. Some people reported not being able to sleep for days. Needless to say, when night finally returned, the whole town took a long nap.

According to NASA, the event was caused by a "solar flare-induced atmospheric reflection." A write up in the paper described how such an event occurs when a massive and highly charged solar flare interacts with Earth's magnetosphere, ionizing the upper atmosphere in a certain way. The ionization creates a reflective layer that refracts sunlight around the planet, effectively eliminating night by scattering light across the sky continuously. An interesting theory.

However, there were conflicting reports that said the week of sunlight was caused by an axial shift of the Earth due to "an unknown celestial event," for example, a rogue planet closely passing by. Others said it was a solar reflection caused by a giant alien structure in outer space, or that it was a "time dilation bubble"—which I never bothered to ask about. The explanations satisfied everyone else. I found them curiously insufficient.

However, I've also made some of my own observations about New Hinton that I would categorize as oddities. I can't really say whether they are inherent to New Hinton or not because I've never traveled beyond the city's parameters—nor has anyone I know. The foreigner I met at the bookstore is the only outsider I ever encountered.

One peculiar observation is how certain people, even animals, sometimes appear to be repeating the same task, as if stuck in a loop. It can be bewildering, like the way the same bluejay always swoops down, just missing the tip of our garden fountain at exactly quarter-past eight every morning. Or how the mailman always takes exactly three steps back after putting the mail through the door slot—small things you wouldn't necessarily notice, but where you might recognize a certain pattern, if you know what I mean.

Once I began noticing patterns, it became difficult to stop. There's a young kid, Timmy, that delivers our newspaper on an old Schwinn with large canvas bags full of folded papers tied to the handlebars, and he always seems to be in one of these "loops." It's not just the method in which he delivers the paper—after all, tedious, repetitious work lends itself to patterns—it's the way he goes from house to house doing his monthly collection.

I've watched him several times and he always behaves the same way after collecting his check: he turns around, walks to the end of the driveway, removes his cap, wipes his brow with the back of his left hand, looks at the ground for a few seconds, and then grabs his bike and goes on to the next house.

He never deviates.

He also seems to be easily thrown-off by inconsistencies, like when the neighbor's Pomeranian got out and began chewing on his pant leg. To the neighbor's astonishment, Timmy just got on his bike and started pedaling—as if nothing had happened! The neighbor had to get in her car, find him, and then plead with him to stop in order to get her snowy white "Princess," marked with chain grease, back. Needless to say, she canceled her subscription soon after.

When I've mentioned my hypothesis about Timmy to my parents, they always tell me to stop being so critical. *Do not judge, or you too will be judged. For in the same way you judge others, you will be judged, and with the measure you use, it will be measured to you.* Just one of the many biblical phrases Mom likes to use in order to make her point.

Regardless, one day I decided to put Timmy to a little test. I saw him approaching our house to make his monthly collection, and I let Mom answer the door. As they were talking about the weather or something, I ran out the same door, said "Hi" to Timmy, and then bent down next to him as if my shoe lace had come undone. At the same time I was pretending to tie my shoe, I untied his. I then proceeded to walk across the street and hide behind a parked Buick to see what would happen next.

After Mom and Timmy had finished their small talk and Timmy got his check, he did the usual: he turned around, walked to the end of the driveway, removed his cap, wiped his brow with the back of his left hand, and looked at the ground for a few seconds. But when he noticed his shoe was untied, he appeared perplexed and stood for what seemed like an entire minute just looking at it. He then began to slowly walk in circles, stamping the foot with the untied shoe, like some kind of injured animal. This continued for a while until something clicked, and he had the wherewithal to bend down and tie the shoelace.

My conclusion was that, unlike the Pomeranian, this little diversion had the effect of breaking the loop, which inevitably left him searching for an appropriate response that he couldn't find. I thought about doing a follow-up test, just to confirm my theory that he really was in a loop, but I didn't have the heart to follow through with it. I mean, maybe he was just weird like that? Anyway, if anyone found out what I was doing, they might think I was mocking him (which wasn't my intention, I was just curious). Nevertheless, I had to be careful, especially being vulnerable to ridicule myself. In the end, I promised myself that I would be extra kind to Timmy the next time I saw him.

However, Timmy isn't the only one who has driven me to wonder about such things. All around me, I've noticed a certain rhythm to everyday life in New Hinton. It's in the way the school bus driver always arrives perfectly on time, not a minute too early or too late. The way the checkout girl at the hardware store always greets us with the same "How are you today? Did you find everything you were looking for?" Or the way the firemen are only seen when there is an emergency, and then mysteriously disappear into their residence, never to be seen again until the next one.

Just last week, the aging mayor of New Hinton was giving a speech in front of the press and froze on live TV with his mouth left gaping, as if someone had pulled his plug. An aide had to gently walk him back to his office, like a mother guiding her child. People were saying he had a mini-stroke, and yet, the next day I saw him coming out of the post office by himself, perfectly fine.

Then, there is the peculiar woman who works at the pharmacy, downtown. Last week I decided to drop in because they always have a good selection of magazines, including my favorite—*Mad Magazine.* When I discovered they had the latest edition, I asked her how much it was with tax, and she oddly replied, "Be careful to take it only once a day, and never before bed."

Confused, I looked around, just in case she was talking to someone else, but there was nobody else in the store. So I brought the magazine to the counter and asked her again. She then said—without a hint of irony—"Young man, I'm afraid I can't let you purchase this without a prescription from your doctor." I was waiting for her to break out into laughter and tell me it was all a joke, but she just stood there, staring at me with a pleasant smile. Puzzled, I gently set the magazine on the counter and walked out. "Have a nice day!" I could hear her say behind me. I told myself it was nothing. Still, something in me remained unsettled.

Sometimes, I doubt myself and think I'm being overly suspicious and conspiratorial, and trying too hard to make something out of nothing. My mom says I shouldn't be asking so many questions or trying to be too smart. I think it's strange how she warns me that over-analyzing things will only "lead to your own self-destruction"—whatever that means. But I can't help myself. Those who seek the truth do so because they must. For us, it's not a choice whether or not to seek the truth. In the end, I didn't know what I was searching for —only that I could no longer ignore the questions.

Leaving Home

The night before I left, I had a strange dream.

It began in the most mundane of places: in the bathroom of my parent's house. I was washing my face, when I looked in the mirror and noticed an unruly thick nose hair sticking out of my nostril like a weed stubbornly pushing through cracked pavement. So, I grabbed the tweezers and gave it a good yank. However, pulling on it only revealed more of it. As I continued to pull, the hair extended further out from my nose, curling almost like a root. Shocked that such a thing could have come out of my body, I searched for some scissors to snip the unwieldy thing, but I wasn't able to cut it with the small pair I found in the bathroom drawer.

The dream ended shortly after my mom burst into the bathroom, her face a mix of concern and urgency, and began to frantically push it back up my nose. There was no explanation, no comfort—just a sense of helplessness, as if we were both trapped in a situation we couldn't understand, trying to reverse something that should have never been.

I decided to make my departure shortly after everyone went to bed. That way, I would be able to cover some distance before anyone noticed I was gone and started looking for me. I packed lightly, putting only an extra sweater and a flashlight in an old backpack. Before I left, I placed a note on the kitchen table for my family. I would've liked to explain everything to my parents in person, but what they wanted for me isn't what I wanted. It's not really their fault, they just wanted what all parents want for their children—for them to be happy, safe, and grow to be independent. But none of that mattered to me. Even though I had finished high school, I had little interest in anything other than finding the truth about what I experienced that summer afternoon as a child.

Memories had been lingering for years, like a fire smoldering in the back of my mind. In spite of the profoundness of the event, at the time, I was still too young to turn it into any kind of earnest quest for self-knowledge. But now that I was older and finished with high school, I had decided it was time to explore the world and see what, if any, answers it might provide. The last thing I wanted to do was go to college and try to be serious about my studies. Either way—college or not—I figured, I would end up disappointing my parents. College could wait. For now, I was on a journey.

Leaving home without telling anyone was harder than I thought it would be. I imagined it would pain my family dearly to not know where I had gone. My mom would blame herself for not raising me properly. On the other hand, my dad would mostly deflect any sense of guilt by suggesting they should've sent me to a councilor soon after the event. But my inner compass was strong. It's what gave me the strength that night to quietly go through the garage, leave through the side door, and then slowly and carefully open the gate leading to the front yard—making sure it didn't creek too loudly in the dampened night air.

The next step of my plan was to simply walk out of New Hinton. However, I had to admit, I wasn't even sure if it was possible. Nobody I knew had ever traveled beyond New Hinton, nor expressed any desire to do so. What would I find? Is there even a "getting out" of New Hinton, I wondered, or is it spherical so that walking in a straight line will eventually bring me back to where I began? That would explain why nobody ever left New Hinton, or thought about leaving it. Also, could such a physical limitation result in a mental limitation, such that nobody could imagine 'out'? Perhaps I was the first one to even consider that there was something beyond New Hinton. Of course, if that were the case, it would be the end of my quest. I would be leaving, not realizing that my destination is where I was already standing.

I tried to ignore my racing, inquisitive thoughts, including the one about whether or not this was all a terrible idea. If I hesitated, I thought, I might turn back—and I couldn't afford that. So I kept walking ahead. Mile after mile, pressing forward, avoiding the main roads, and keeping to the shadows where I could. If anyone were looking for me, I didn't want to make it easy for them.

By my rough estimates, I had already covered about twenty miles, pausing only for short breaks to rest my aching legs. As I left New Hinton behind, the sounds of the city begin to fade. The further I go, the quieter it gets—until all that remains is an eerie, distant humming sound, low and droning, just on the edge of perception. I can't tell where it's coming from, but it follows me, like an under-current beneath the silence.

The houses grow sparse. The streetlights become fewer and farther between, flickering like dying embers. The roads narrow, the pavement cracks and crumbles until it's more dirt than asphalt. I have no real sense of direction—only a singular goal: out. I walk straight ahead and yet, part of me still wonders if in a day or two I'll end up back at my own doorstep.

As night falls, I veer off a lonely country road to look for a place to rest out of view from any drivers. I push through the underbrush, my steps slow and careful. The night air is still, thick with the scent of damp earth. I'm just looking for a place to rest, somewhere out of sight until morning. That's when I see it—a small, squat structure, half-hidden beneath a tangle of vines. At first, I think it's an old storage shed, maybe even the remnants of a farmhouse. But as I get closer, I notice the way the concrete is smoothed, reinforced, different from the weathered wood of nearby ruins.

I shine my flashlight over the entrance. There's a metal door, slightly ajar, rust creeping along its edges. It doesn't look like anyone's been here in a long time. I hesitate for a moment, then step forward and push it open.

Inside, the air is stale but not suffocating. My flashlight sweeps over shelves lined with canned food, neatly stacked but long expired. A few plastic containers sit in the corner, sealed tight, their labels faded with age. Someone had prepared for something here—but whatever it was, they either didn't need it or never made it back.

I move further in, trailing my fingers lightly over the dusty surfaces. There's nothing overtly strange about the place—it's just an old bunker, likely built decades ago. But then I notice the odd mix of objects on a nearby table.

A thin, rectangle of dark glass lies among a pile of scattered papers. I pick it up, turning it over in my hands. It's smooth, heavier than it looks. It doesn't have any buttons, any markings—just a single faint crack along one side. It feels strange, almost deliberate in its simplicity, but I have no idea what it is. I set it back down and turn my attention to the supplies.

The shelves are lined with vacuum-sealed food packs, labeled with plain, functional text: "Soy Protein Ration – Fortified," "Hydration Pack – Electrolyte Blend," "Nutrient Paste – Multi-Vitamin Formula." The packaging is unfamiliar, sleek, and minimalist—far different from the canned goods that have long since rusted. I pick up one of the packs and turn it over. The print on the back reads:

ISSUED: 04-23-2041

I pause.

2041?

That doesn't make sense. I quickly do the calculation. How could it have been issued sixty-five years in the future?

I set the pack down and continue looking. A large, unopened case of water bottles sits in one corner, the labels still intact. Unlike anything I've seen before, the bottles are thicker, with a built-in filtration system inside the cap. Further back, I spot a stack of metal canisters labeled "Oxygen Reserve – Portable Use." I hesitate, picking one up. Why would anyone need portable oxygen in a place like this?

Near the back wall, a heavy-duty backpack rests against a stack of plastic storage bins. I unzip it and find a small first aid kit, compact but well-stocked—antiseptic wipes, syringes pre-loaded with some kind of medication, and a tiny, folded instruction sheet written in both English and another language I don't recognize.

A case of books sits nearby, stacked neatly beside the backpack. I crouch down and pull one out, running my fingers over the cover. The title is unfamiliar—not a novel, not a history book, but something technical, something about preservation science and human psychology.

I flip through a few pages, but the contents don't make much sense to me—diagrams of long-term storage units, mention of a "cryo-stasis chamber," and notes on "psychological adjustments for extended habitation." I frown and tuck it back into the case.

I take a final glance around. Whoever stocked this place wasn't just preparing for a storm or a short-term crisis. They were preparing for something much bigger—something long-term. But in spite of its original purpose, I find there's something peaceful about the old bunker. Maybe it's just me enjoying some undisturbed time away. I begin to think I could stay here a while. In the stillness of this place I might find a steadiness that has eluded me for some time.

I grab a dusty blanket from one of the shelves, shake it out, and settle into a corner, using my backpack as a pillow. The night is quiet, save for the faint sound of the wind outside.

As I close my eyes, my thoughts drift.

It's strange, though—2041.

For a moment, I wonder what kind of world existed back then— what kind of future this place came from. But sleep comes quickly, and the thought fades with it.

At the Edge of the World

I wake before dawn, still curious about the bunker, but determined to make the most of the morning while my energy is high. The miles slip by beneath my feet, each step carrying me farther from New Hinton, deeper into the unknown. My watch says it's almost noon and yet, the sky has a strange darkening to it as if I'm looking at the seam in the sky where day meets night. Behind me is the mid-day sun, and ahead of me is twilight. There are only a few thin clouds above, and they appear static. There is no wind and nothing moves—except, strangely, the treetops. It's unsettling, as if I were about to reach the edge of the world.

The humming I faintly experienced since I left New Hinton has now grown into a low, resonant thrum—a pulse like the heartbeat of something massive and unseen. I enter through a dense grove of tall eucalyptus trees which is so dark I need to use my flashlight. Their towering tree tops are swaying unnaturally in the still air. When I come out the other end, I discover a vast, barren clearing, where the humming is now loud enough, I can feel it in my chest.

Scattered before me are dozens of uniform, self-operating, windowless buildings. Each is surrounded by its own chain-linked fence topped with razor-sharp barbed wire.

No movement, no signs of human presence.

My flashlight lands on the nearest structure. A small, flickering light barely illuminates a fading identification number cracked and peeling with age:

"Pod 3 A1-623"

Just below it is a steel door, reinforced and seamless, as if designed to withstand more than just the elements. There is no door handle, just a vent near the bottom. A sign, rusted at the edges and bolted to the door's surface, warns:

"Keep out. Authorized personnel only."

The scattered structures give way to an immense wall rising like an unmoving sentinel, so dark it nearly merges with the sky. It dwarfs everything around it—forty feet at least, maybe more. Its surface is seamless, with no doors or windows, no obvious purpose—only an unyielding boundary that seems to have always been there.

As I trace the wall's edge into the distance, I realize it doesn't run straight—it curves subtly left and right. A gut-churning suspicion settles in: it may encircle far more than I can see, stretching beyond the limits of my perception. I have no idea what lies behind it, only the sense that this boundary marks the edge of something immense.

The surface feels unfamiliar—cold and unnaturally smooth, like polished stone or some synthetic alloy. It doesn't yield to my touch. I withdraw my hand, unsettled.

Behind it, barely visible through a low mist, rise massive industrial towers, jagged against the darkened sky. Their angular metal

forms are wrapped in thick ventilation ducts, their surfaces filmed
with peeling grime. From their tops, black conduits snake across
the skyline like twisted arteries, crisscrossing and converging
toward a purpose I can't begin to understand.

The air has changed. This cold isn't the chill of night or moving
wind—it feels deeper, unnatural. A heaviness clings to my skin, and
the sharp smell of dust and rusting metal fills my lungs.

I try to focus, to make sense of the scattered buildings before me,
searching for some clue—some trace of purpose. But the facades
are monotonous, stripped of character, offering nothing but impersonal surfaces.

The noise comes from everywhere at once—a low, mechanical
breathing that surrounds me. Beneath it, a sharp hiss releases at
intervals, as if pressure is being bled from something immense. I
fight the urge to cover my ears.

The ground beneath me trembles with an energy felt more than
seen. Subtle vibrations ripple upward through my feet. In places
the earth gives way, exposing large corroded pipes once buried deep
below. Strange vents rise from the ground nearby, lending the landscape an almost biological feel.

Taken together, the sound, the steel, and the stale metallic air
leave me with the unmistakable sense that I have entered the
belly of something vast and alive—a mechanical beast slumbering
beneath the earth. This place does not feel meant to be seen. And
yet here I stand, too close for comfort, at the edge of something far
beyond my understanding.

Curious to learn more, I find what looks like an underground
entrance—a hatch fitted with a heavy wheel like something from
a submarine or bank vault. With effort, the rusted wheel begins to
turn. At that exact moment, a strange flying object whirs past and

hovers briefly overhead. I can't make it out in the dim light, but it moves like a giant dragonfly. It's the only creature I've encountered here.

As the hatch groans open, a rush of stale metallic air escapes, carrying the scent of dampness and something faintly electric—like the aftershock of lightning. My pulse quickens. It feels as though I've disturbed something long forgotten.

I peer down into the shaft. The concrete tube descends beyond sight, swallowed by the dim glow of flickering lights set into the walls. A corroded metal ladder clings to the side. The air is thick, heavy with age, and I hesitate, my fingers tightening on the hatch's cold rim.

Above, the strange flying creature returns, circling once before vanishing into the darkness, its presence lingering in the back of my mind. The stillness down below is almost oppressive, but something in me stirs, a deep pull urging me forward.

I grip the first rung of the ladder and step inside. The metal creaks under my weight. The dim light shimmers faintly against the concrete, illuminating flecks of dust that drift lazily in the stale air. Every movement echoes, amplifying the isolation.

The shaft comes down into what appears to be a transportation tunnel of some kind. I continue to descend until my feet touch down on a grated metal floor. Dim recessed lighting flickers along the curved walls, revealing the sheer scale of the space. The tunnel isn't just a simple passage—it's industrial, built for something bigger than just passenger transit.

In front of me stretches a single rail, its surface smooth and unbroken, humming faintly with residual power. A narrow walkway runs parallel, bordered by small, periodic maintenance stations, their access panels sealed shut. The infrastructure is intact, but there's something unsettling about its sterility. No debris. No clutter. Just an absolute silence that makes my thoughts appear even louder.

I start walking, my footsteps muted against the metal path. Despite the tunnel's apparent age, there's no sign of decay, no rust, no organic overgrowth. If anything, it feels… maintained. That thought freaks me out. Who is keeping it intact?

To fight off a sense of apprehension, I tell myself no matter what happens, I'm not going back, and I continue walking. After what feels like miles, a warm glow appears ahead, distinct from the cold blue tunnel lights.

As I draw closer, the space opens up into a platform—but not the kind built for people. The platform is long and utilitarian, with reinforced staging areas and massive loading bays lining one side. There are no benches, no passenger schedules, no signs directing travelers. Instead, heavy-duty scaffolding, supply crates, and the remains of large docking clamps hint that the platform's original purpose was some kind of a logistics hub.

Beyond the platform, I notice a row of glass-fronted offices, their interiors visible through the dust-covered panels. The rooms beyond are eerily preserved, as if abandoned mid-task. Desks remain cluttered with blueprints, screens frozen on engineering models, and half-empty coffee cups turned into brittle relics.

As I step inside, my sleeve brushes against a layer of dust—a detail that doesn't quite fit. In contrast to the pristine tunnel and platform, here entropy has been allowed to settle.

Next, I see what I can only describe as some kind of holographic display, like the one used in Star Wars. Sitting dormant on the main desk, its last projection is flickering faintly—technical schematics of an underground structure glitching before collapsing into a static image.

Pinned to the wall, a progress timeline stops abruptly. The last logged entry reads:

"Finalization complete. Handoff initiated."

"Handoff of what and to whom?" I wonder out loud. I look for a date that would reveal more, and incomprehensibly find it written:

"June 15, 2045"

Have I somehow been ported to the future? Like my experience with the items found in the old bunker, none of this makes sense. I glance around. The entire station—this whole system—feels like it should be in use, but the human presence has long gone.

I check one of the old control panels, pressing a few buttons at random.

Nothing.

The system doesn't appear to be offline, but doesn't respond. That's when I notice, at the far end of the platform, a train stands motionless.

It isn't covered in dust. It doesn't look abandoned.

It looks… ready.

Eastborough

I step cautiously toward the motionless train. Its sleek, angular design is different from any transit system I am familiar with. There are no windows, only a smooth, metallic exterior that reflects the dim light from the platform. The doors are sealed shut, but as I get closer, a faint hiss of hydraulics breaks the silence, and they slide open with utmost precision.

Inside, the train is eerily pristine—not abandoned, but untouched. The walls are lined with rows of contoured seats, each embedded with dormant TV-like screens. There are no manual controls—only an empty space where a conductor's panel might have been.

As soon as I cross the threshold, the doors seal shut behind me, and without warning, the train comes to life. A soft blue glow pulses along the interior walls, and the cabin gently vibrates as the rail engages. I barely have time to find a seat before the train accelerates smoothly, silently, the platform outside vanishing within seconds into darkness.

The speed is disorienting. There's no traditional sensation of movement—no lurching, no rattling of tracks. The entire experience is frictionless, like gliding through empty space. The interior remains silent except for the soft hum of the rail underneath. Then, faintly, a voice—not spoken aloud, but coming from the interface embedded in the nearest seat. The display flickers to life with a single line of text:

DESTINATION: POD 4, SECTOR 33

A map blinks onto the screen, showing a sprawling network of underground tunnels—my current location, marked as a tiny blue dot, is traveling toward a larger hub several miles away. The display shifts again. A status update appears:

"Passenger acknowledged. Transit in progress. Estimated arrival: 14:12:23."

Passenger? A chill runs through my spine. I hadn't interacted with the system at all—yet it recognized me. The train continues through the vast tunnel system, passing through intermittent flashes of dim emergency lighting. Occasionally, the tunnel walls reveal glimpses of side corridors, sealed maintenance doors, or branching routes leading elsewhere.

I watch the display, waiting for more information, but the system remains silent. It doesn't ask for confirmation, doesn't prompt for interaction. It already knows where I'm going.

Then, just as suddenly as it started, the train begins to decelerate. The transition is seamless. As the train slows, the dark tunnel outside gives way to another platform, larger than the first. The architecture is different—more advanced, more refined. Whatever this place was meant for, it was built at a later stage in development.

The doors slide open. The platform is empty. Unlike the abandoned station before, this place still appears functional. The air is fresher, the lighting more consistent, the walls free of dust and decay. It feels occupied, even though no one is here. Ahead, a corridor branches off from the platform, leading deeper into the facility. This isn't just another transit stop—it's an entrance. To what, I don't yet know.

A soft chime sounds from behind me. The train doors remain open, waiting, as if expecting me to step off. I feel I have no choice but to leave the train and confront whatever is at the other end of this terminal. I take a few cautious steps into the long, winding corridor ahead. The walls are functional, lined with reinforced plating and embedded lighting strips, similar to the tunnels I passed earlier.

Scuff marks, tire treads, and faint traces of grime and dust buildup along the edges of the floor suggest that freight has moved through this space recently. This corridor was—and still might be—used for transporting materials. As I walk, the passage twists and turns, climbing gradually.

The corridor eventually leads to a flight of metal stairs, the first real architectural shift from the underground facility. I ascend cautiously, my footsteps echoing against the hollow steps. At the top, a thick industrial door stands slightly ajar. Pale, natural light filters through the opening—a stark contrast to the artificial glow I've been following.

Pushing through, I emerge into a vast, empty warehouse. The ceiling is high, lined with suspended light fixtures. Rows of abandoned shipping containers and freight pallets sit in neat alignment, as if they were left in the middle of distribution. A few have logistics labels with strange symbols, some of which I don't recognize.

At the far end of the warehouse, a wide loading dock stands open, revealing a sliver of the outside world. Beyond it, a suburban landscape stretches into the distance. Rows of buildings, roads, and quiet streets—eerily familiar, yet distinctly different.

As I step outside, I realize something unsettling: I haves no idea where I am.

I walk through the grid-like industrial area, which eventually gives way to something looser, more organic. The streets now are wider, dustier, and lined with buildings that don't quite match in height or style. Some are modern but weathered, while others look cobbled together from repurposed materials. There's no strict uniformity here, no sense of rigid urban planning like New Hinton.

I see unpaved side streets, where strings of colorful lights crisscross above open-air cafés and taverns. The sidewalks are cracked in places, but no one seems to mind. The people here move at a slower, more deliberate pace—not sluggish, but unhurried, as if they aren't constantly keeping track of time.

Murals and hand-painted signs cover the walls. Some depict abstract shapes and symbols, others feature quotes or poetic phrases, many of which I'm not familiar with. A few make me pause, like one scrawled in fading paint outside a bookshop:

"Time is a mirror, and we are the hands that touch its surface."

There's a warmth to the town, but also a strangeness. It's not just the physical differences from New Hinton—it's the way the people interact, the way they regard me with open curiosity but not suspicion.

I step into a central square, which isn't exactly a traditional town center. Instead of a courthouse or towering office buildings, there's a communal space—an open-air market mixed with cafés, bars, and makeshift outdoor bookstores. A group of people sit cross-legged near an old stone fountain, engaged in deep conversation. One of them gestures animatedly, speaking about something I can't quite hear. A street musician plays an instrument I don't recognize—stringed, but the sound is eerily resonant, almost meditative. A small stall sells hand-bound books, many without titles, as if the covers are meant to be inscribed by the reader. At a café with wooden benches and vines creeping up the walls, a chalkboard menu features a drink called "The Lucid Blend"—whatever that means.

The people dress in a way that feels both old and new—practical yet expressive. Some wear loose, flowing clothes; others mix old-world styles with modern fabrics. I immediately notice more beards, more long hair, more scarves and jewelry made from natural materials. The people carry a certain energy—one that seems more self-directed, less constrained by the expectations of a traditional society.

I hesitate, scanning the town square for something—anything—that might further lead me in my journey. Then, I spot him—a boy about my age, leaning against the edge of a stone fountain, watching me with quiet curiosity. He has dark, unruly hair and wears a simple linen shirt, the sleeves rolled up to his elbows.

"You're not from this place," he says, tilting his head slightly.

"Why are you here?"

I hesitate, then exhale. "I'm not sure."

The boy studies me for a moment, then nods. "You're looking for something."

I blink. "I guess so."

He smiles slightly. "So, what are you looking for?"

I hesitate. I've been asked variations of this question before, but somehow, coming from him, it feels sharper, more precise—less like curiosity and more like a test.

"I don't know," I admit. "I just know there's something I need to understand."

He exhales through his nose, something between a laugh and a sigh. "Yeah, I've met guys like you before."

"Guys like me?"

"The spiritual seekers." He gestures vaguely at me. "You think you're different from everyone else. You're not. The others just follow their routine, and so do you—except yours is more complicated and you dress it up as a 'journey.'"

A flicker of annoyance rises in me. "That's not true."

"Isn't it?" He cocks his head, sizing me up. "You came here thinking you'd find something, didn't you? Maybe a wise old man who would pat you on the head and hand you an 'Enlightenment Certificate'?"

I narrow my eyes. "That's not what I—"

He cuts me off. "Then what? What do you actually expect to happen? That one day, some hidden door in your mind will swing open and—boom!—you'll finally get it?"

His words hit harder than I expect. I clench my jaw, trying to brush them off. "You wouldn't understand."

He raises an eyebrow. "Wouldn't I?"

There's something about the way he says it that makes me pause. He's testing me, waiting to see if I'll push back.

I exhale through my nose, the tension simmering. "Do you always test people like this?"

He grins. "It's a gift." Then, after a pause, he adds, "Name's Rohan, by the way."

"Vic," I reply automatically.

Rohan smirks. "Nice to meet you, Vic. Even if you're a lost cause."

I roll my eyes. "And here I thought you were warming up to me."

Rohan shrugs. "You remind me of someone. He didn't know what the hell he was looking for either."

I tilt my head. "What happened to him?"

Rohan grins. "He figured it out. But he hated the answer."

For a moment, we just stand there, neither of us speaking. The tension lingers, but something about it feels cleaner—like the air after a storm.

Rohan gestures toward a narrow street leading away from the square. "Come on. If you're still set on playing this game, I'll take you to someone who can mess with your head better than I can."

I hesitate, then nod, not having anywhere else to go.

We walk in silence for a while. But something about the quiet between us has changed. It's not quite trust, but it's something.

We leave the town square and weave through the narrow streets, past hand-carved wooden doors and walls covered in ivy. The deeper we go, the quieter the town becomes, until we reach a modest building at the edge of a small garden with dozens of pairs of shoes and sandals sitting outside the door.

"We're in luck," Rohan says, "Adi is doing his usual afternoon question-and-answer."

I step through the doorway, uncertain of what awaits me. Inside, a diverse group of people is gathered in a small room, sitting casually on the floor, some on cushions. They seem to come from all walks of life—some resembling the spiritual seekers I've read about, while others have the air of intellectuals. A few lean forward intently, jotting down notes like eager students hanging on a professor's every word, while others sit in a relaxed, meditative posture, eyes gently closed, trying to absorb the moment, as if by osmosis.

At the end of the room, an old man sits cross-legged on a low, covered platform, his gaze calm yet piercing. I was expecting someone, perhaps, in silk robes, lighting incense, but he appears no different than any other man I've encountered on the street here. He looks…well…ordinary, like a street vendor; that is, nothing remarkable at first glance.

On one side of him is a fan running, sitting on top of a folded newspaper, stirring the warm air, and on the other side is a devotee wearing thick glasses with a cassette player resting in his hands, capturing the teacher's words for posterity.

The walls of the room are lined with what appear to be framed pictures of saints, or perhaps venerated teachers. Other than that, there is no furniture except for two folding chairs occupied by an older couple in the back. Two open windows provide lighting and ventilation, thinly veiled by drapes. And there's a stairwell that leads up to a second floor, which, I assume, is the residency of the old man.

He studies me for a moment and then gestures for me to sit on the floor. There is no room, but he insists, and asks the group to make space for me at the very front, which causes an interruption as the group shifts and realigns itself. Nevertheless, people are accommodating and don't appear annoyed by the disturbance. I would've preferred to have stayed in the back where I could just observe and not be observed, but that's no longer an option.

Next, someone politely reminds me to remove my shoes. I do so and take them outside. When I come back in, I nervously make my way to the front, trying hard not to step on any fingers or toes. I take a seat on the cold, hard floor, a bit tense to be rubbing shoulders with those sitting so close next to me.

"Now, what were you saying?" asks the old man waving at a woman sitting at the center of the room. Her dreadlock hair lumped like a mound on top of her head is absolutely primeval. In contrast, her face appears as soft and rosy as a baby's.

"I can't accept this idea that the world is just 'play'," she says in a serious tone.

The teacher watches her for a moment before responding.

"What's wrong with 'play'? I think you're looking for it to have some kind of purpose. Only those who feel they are lacking something need purpose. Until you feel complete, perfecting 'you' will always be the purpose. Am I right?"

The woman's expression tightens some more, as if she knows he's right but refuses to acknowledge it.

The old man continues, "But if someday you find yourself complete and not lacking anything, then you will actually begin to enjoy the world and won't feel it to be a burden. To others, you might appear to be working hard in the world, making a living and dealing with family problems like everyone else, but that is only what it looks like," he says before providing an example. "Football players on a field appear to be working hard too, but they know it's all just a game; that it's all just sport."

She shakes her head. "Are you suggesting that the universe is just about having a good time?"

The teacher exhales softly, his patience unwavering.

"The universe is perfect as it is," he says. "The universe is not only perfect, it's beautiful. It has beauty, which it creates for the sheer pleasure of it."

"So, then, beauty is its purpose!" the woman presses.

The teacher, now visually agitated, leans back slightly. "Enough with this talk about purpose! Why does the world need to have purpose? Purpose implies that it needs to be corrected, that something is not right. The universe's aim isn't beauty, the universe is beauty. Does a rose try to be beautiful? No, it just is. By its own nature it's beautiful! In the same way, the universe is perfection itself without any effort on its part."

Next, the woman tries to make it all tie together somehow, "My understanding is purpose completes itself via beauty."

"How do you define 'beauty'?" shoots back the teacher, now raising his voice. "Isn't it bliss that is the essence of beauty?"

"That I am is obvious. That I perceive is obvious. That I am happiness, well,…"

"If *I am* were obvious, you wouldn't have to worry about being happy, because you would know you are happiness. But because you are distracted by what you aren't, and can't stay focused on what you are, you miss being happy." He pauses before waving his hand to show he's done with her question.

I feel like it's the first day of high school and I've mistakenly wandered into the advanced calculus class. Unfortunately, there is no running for the exits.

"You," pointing at me, "Who are you?"

I blink. "Um, my name is Victor." I turn behind me timidly to acknowledge the others. "Thank you for having me."

"You're 'Victor-thank-you-for-having-me'?" asks the old man.

A few in the room snicker quietly.

I shift awkwardly, "No, no, just Victor. My friends call me Vic, actually."

"But who are you?" he repeats.

I am bewildered by the question and don't know how to respond.

"Um, I just told you, I'm…"

"WHO. ARE. YOU." he repeats, with emphasis on each word.

I pause long enough to gain my composure before telling him, "With all due respect, but shouldn't the question be, 'What am I?'"

The old man leans back and flashes a rare grin at the devotee sitting next to him.

"Good, good," he says seemingly pleased. "So, then, what are you?"

"Well, I don't know. That's what I want to find out." And then, for whatever reason—maybe it is being far away from home, or maybe because I am nervous—I just off-load everything I had been carrying with me: "You see I'm on a bit of a quest after I had this kind of death experience when I was younger but couldn't make much sense of it and learned a lot about myself but still don't understand everything from it and so I ran away from home and then encountered this strange underground train that eventually brought me here and now I'm here but really don't know where I am and frankly…I'm a bit lost." I take a breath and try to slow down. "So, not only do I not know who—or better—what I am, I don't know where I am." And then I finish with an abrupt, "Did that answer your question?"

Silence.

At the same time, I feel another death experience coming on—or at least the desire to have one.

I brace myself, expecting the old man to lash out or, at the very least, send me to the back of the room. But next, his piercing gaze—the kind that breaks through ignorance like an ice pick—softens and transforms into a vast ocean of compassion.

"Well then, welcome to Eastborough. I'm sorry the journey was so long and arduous for you. I hope you find what you're looking for. In the meantime, my assistant in the back can help you find a place to stay."

I respond with my palms together and a deep bow—something I have never done before but feel compelled to do all the same out of profound gratitude. You see, it wasn't only what the old teacher said, but what I felt he had transmitted. I can't describe it, I have never felt so…cared for, not even by my own family. It felt like the universe had directly spoken to me. My eyes begin to well up as I feel the happiness the old man briefly spoke of before.

After the talk, I linger near the doorway, the energy of the room still clinging to me. The assistant—Susan, I think her name was—gives me a kind smile and asks if I'd like assistance finding a place to lodge at. I hesitate, glancing back at the gathering, the quiet hum of conversation filling the space.

For a moment, I almost say yes. I could stay here for a while. Let everything settle. Try to make sense of what just happened. But the restlessness is already creeping back in.

I shake my head. "Thank you, but I think I should keep moving."

She studies me for a beat, then nods as if she expected that answer. "If you change your mind, you know where to find us."

Outside, the evening air is cool, and the city feels different now—not less alive, but more calm. Lanterns flicker in the marketplace, casting long, shifting shadows across the cobblestone streets.

Adi, the old teacher is waiting for me.

I pause when I see him standing at the edge of the garden, hands clasped behind his back. He regards me with that same knowing expression he held during the talk—like he sees more than what's in front of him.

"You are not staying," he says.

It isn't a question.

I shake my head. "No."

He nods, as if confirming something for himself. "There is a town, just beyond the hills," he says. "Sundarville. Go there in the morning."

The name is unfamiliar. "What's in Sundarville?"

The old man smiles faintly. "Many more who can help you."

I frown. "Help me with what?"

His eyes glint with something unreadable. "That is for you to find out."

I exhale slowly, rubbing the back of my neck. I could push him for more, but I get the feeling it wouldn't do any good. Whatever he means by help, it isn't something he plans on explaining.

He glances toward the street. "Rohan will take you."

I turn my head just as Rohan steps out of the shadows, arms crossed, watching me like he's already bored of whatever is about to happen next.

I let out a short breath. "Of course he will."

The teacher only smiles.

Rohan steps forward, giving the old man a small, respectful nod before turning to me. "Looks like we're traveling together now."

I shake my head, smirking slightly. "I was about to say the same thing."

The teacher places a gentle hand on my shoulder. It's a brief touch, but something in it steadies me. There's a weight to him— not physical, but something deeper. Like his presence alone anchors me for a moment before I drift away again.

The old man steps back, his gaze soft but firm. Then, without another word, he turns and disappears into the house, the door creaking softly as it closes behind him.

The silence that follows is heavier than I expect.

Rohan lets out a sigh. "Well. That was mysterious as hell."

I huff a quiet laugh. "Yeah."

He jerks his head toward the street. "Find a place to sleep. We leave at first light."

The first hints of dawn are just beginning to touch the rooftops of Eastborough when I step outside. The streets are nearly empty, save for a few early risers setting up their stalls in the marketplace. The air is crisp and still, the remnants of night clinging to the city like a thin veil.

Rohan is waiting for me by the fountain, arms crossed, watching the town slowly wake up.

"Ready?" he asks.

I glance around one last time.

For a moment, I think about staying.

The teacher's words, the warmth of the gathering, the feeling of having a place where I could belong if I let myself—all of it pulls at me, just for a second.

Then I take a step forward.

And I don't look back.

Charlatans and Sages

Rohan leads me through the winding roads outside of Eastborough, the path shifting from cobbled streets to dirt-packed trails that stretch into the mist-laden hills. Sundarville emerges through the fog, a town that seems both ancient and untouched, its buildings carved into the hillside, roofs sloping unevenly as if molded by time rather than design.

"This is where I leave you," Rohan says, stopping at the outskirts, his face unreadable. "Be careful, my friend."

Before I can press him for more, he turns and disappears down the trail, his footsteps fading into the quiet. I take a breath and proceed. The town hums low with life, but I feel strangely isolated, even more so than when I first entered Eastborough.

I make my way to a motel where I plan to stay for a few days while I explore Sundarville. The building is unassuming, its wooden facade weathered by time, a neon sign flickering intermittently. As I step toward the entrance, a man—or maybe an older-looking young man—leans casually against the post outside, watching me with a knowing smile.

His clothes are more eccentric than the others I've seen in town—a faded, deep-green velvet coat, mismatched rings on his fingers, and an old leather satchel hanging at his side.

Without waiting for an introduction, he speaks as if he already knows something about me.

"You've got that look," the man says. His voice is smooth, measured. "Like you've stepped through the wrong door and ended up somewhere between a dream and a memory."

I stop.

The man gestures to the empty space beside him. "You don't have to linger. But you should."

Whether this person is a genuine seer, a manipulative charlatan, or just another curious local, I don't know yet.

I hesitate, but the weight of his words holds me in place. There's a strange familiarity about him—something in his posture, in the way his fingers drum absently against the worn leather of his satchel.

Finally, I step forward, keeping a cautious distance. He doesn't turn to face me immediately. Instead, he lets out a soft chuckle, as if amused by my hesitation.

"Sundarville has a way of recognizing those who aren't from here," he says. "It folds around them like a well-worn coat, until they start to believe they belong."

I glance at him, searching his face for clues. Up close, his features are sharp but softened by a kind of agelessness. His deep-green coat looks older than the town itself, its fabric worn at the cuffs. The rings on his fingers glint under the pale neon light, each one different—one plain silver, another etched with symbols I don't recognize.

"And what does Sundarville make of me?" I ask, careful to keep my tone light.

He finally turns to me, his gaze sharp but not unkind. "That depends," he says. "Are you just passing through? Or have you already started to forget where you were headed?"

Something in my chest tightens. I think of the path that led me here—the game, the echoes of childhood that turned too real, the unraveling of everything I thought I understood. And now, this place that feels like a puzzle I was meant to piece together.

"I know where I'm going," I say, though the words don't land as solidly as I'd like.

His smile deepens. "Do you?"

A gust of wind stirs the air, rustling the motel's wooden awning. I notice, now, that the people moving around us never seem to get too close, as if the space we occupy is subtly set apart from the rest of the town.

He leans forward, "Tell me, Vic—"

The sound of my name stops me cold.

I never gave him my name.

My pulse kicks up, but he doesn't press the moment. Instead, he reaches into his satchel and pulls out a small, folded slip of paper. He holds it out to me between two fingers, his expression unreadable.

"Take it," he says. "It's your mantra."

I stare at the paper, my mind already racing with possibilities. Mantra?

The hum of the town presses in around us.

I reach out and take the note.

"Don't share it with anyone. It's only for your eyes."

The paper is smooth but aged, the edges slightly frayed as if it has passed through many hands before mine. I hesitate, feeling the weight of it before unfolding the delicate crease. The words are scrawled in ink, the handwriting uneven yet deliberate.

The dreamer does not dream itself.

The message stirs something deep in me, an unease wrapped in recognition. The letters seem to pulse faintly, or maybe it's just my pulse, heavy in my ears. I glance up at the man, but he only watches, waiting.

"What does it mean?" I ask, my voice quieter than I intended.

He exhales through his nose, something between a sigh and a laugh. "That depends," he says. "Are you ready to see what you've been missing?"

I shake my head. "That's not an answer."

"And yet," he gestures to the paper, "it is."

I look back at the message, tracing the ink with my thumb. The words feel like an invitation—or a warning.

The man leans back, the rings on his fingers clicking softly against one another. "You're at the edge of something, Vic. A threshold. You can walk away, pretend this was nothing more than an odd encounter."

His voice is smooth, too smooth, like someone well-versed in the art of persuasion. There's something rehearsed in his words, the way they coil around me like a carefully placed snare.

His smile lingers, and I see it now—not wisdom, but calculation. A glint in his eyes, not of understanding, but of expectation. He's waiting for me to step forward, waiting for me to commit.

A trick. A performance.

I glance around, my skin prickling. The town still hums with life, but no one meets my gaze. No one acknowledges us. It's as if we've been set apart, deliberately ignored. Or worse—cordoned off.

"You already know," he says again, this time with a knowing smirk, as if amused by my hesitation.

But something in me resists.

The paper in my pocket feels heavier now. The words etched in ink pulse in my mind. The dreamer does not dream itself.

And suddenly, I realize what's wrong. This isn't an invitation. The man isn't offering me knowledge. He's waiting for me to surrender to whatever role he's crafted for me.

I meet his gaze, and for the first time, I see the cracks in his act—the faint tension at the corners of his mouth, the way his fingers tighten around the leather strap of his satchel.

He's not a guide. He's a trap.

And I'm about to fall in.

My breath slows. If I react the way he expects, I'll be caught in whatever web he's spun. I force my body to stay still, my expression unreadable. The game, whatever it is, hinges on me taking the next step. So I don't.

Instead, I let the silence stretch, let the weight of my refusal settle between us. His smirk wavers, just for an instant. A beat too long.

"You're hesitating," he says smoothly, but there's an edge to it now, a note of something almost like impatience.

I shake my head. "No," I say, voice steady. "I'm deciding."

That makes him pause. The rings on his fingers click softly as he adjusts his grip on the satchel. A subtle tell. He's waiting for me to ask a question, to let him guide the conversation, control the flow.

I take a step back instead.

"You want something from me," I say, keeping my tone neutral. "But you haven't told me what."

His smile sharpens, but there's no humor in it. "Haven't I?"

The street around us feels tighter, the space narrowing in a way that isn't quite physical. The town hums low in my ears, the edges of reality blurring just slightly. Whatever this is, it's more than words, more than a con. I need to break free of it.

"You already know," I say, throwing his own words back at him.

And then I turn.

The shift is immediate. The moment I move, the tension between us snaps like a thread pulled too tight. I don't wait to see his reaction—I step toward the motel, my pace even but unhurried, refusing to run.

I count each breath, each footstep, until I reach the door. Only then do I glance back.

He hasn't followed. He's still standing there, watching me, but something in his expression has changed. The smirk is gone.

For the first time, he looks unsure.

I push through the motel door and let it close behind me. The air inside is stale, heavy with the scent of dust and old wood. For the moment, I am safe, but will soon look for other lodging that doesn't attract these kinds of predators just outside its doors.

Weeks pass by and I have taken up residence at a hospice that offers little more than a bed to return to each night. Since I have been here, I've encountered self-proclaimed gurus, teachers who speak in riddles, and spiritual guides more fascinated by their own reflections than by any real wisdom. I've listened to long discourses on enlightenment—on paths and methods, on practices that promise transcendence but deliver only empty rituals. There have been moments of inspiration, brief flashes of insight, but nothing that has led me to what I am truly seeking—a real understanding of what I witnessed that summer day in New Hinton, far away from these exotic whereabouts.

Some teachers have demanded rigid discipline, adherence to techniques that felt mechanical, lifeless. Others have preached indulgence, insisting that detachment means floating through life without responsibility. My restlessness only grows. With each encounter, I feel as though something vital is missing, something that words and techniques can never provide. My patience is running thin.

Then, in a quiet conversation with a wandering monk, I learn of a place at the base of a nearby mountain the locals call *Shroud Peak*. A place where seekers sometimes find more than they expect to. And of a man who does not teach in the usual way. A man who does not claim to know—but simply is. Curiosity leads me there, but skepticism accompanies me—I have been disappointed before.

I set out at dawn, alone, following a narrow dirt path that winds through the outskirts of Sundarville and into the hills beyond. The morning mist clings to the trees, softening the jagged outline of the mountain ahead. The path grows steeper, the town fading behind me, replaced by the rustling of leaves and the distant murmur of a stream.

After hours of walking, I reach a clearing where a handful of people sit in quiet meditation beneath the sprawling limbs of an old oak tree. Their faces are calm, their postures relaxed yet attentive. At the center of the gathering sits a solitary figure.

His presence quiet yet commanding. A simple, white cloth drapes loosely over his thin frame, his feet bare, his eyes half-closed as if straddling the boundary between the seen and the unseen.

I approach cautiously, drawn by an inexplicable pull. This man carries no pretense, no performance—only a stillness that renders the noise of the world irrelevant.

A disciple, a young woman wearing simple clothes, notices me and gestures for me to sit. I hesitate before lowering myself onto the woven mat beside her. The energy in the gathering is unlike anything I have encountered before—calm, unwavering, expectant.

The man, whom they called Arun, lifts his gaze. His eyes meet mine, and for a moment, time seems to collapse inward.

"Who is it that seeks?" Arun's voice was soft yet firm, like a whisper carried by the wind.

Silence settles over the group. No one moves. No one speaks. Yet something profound lingers in the air.

Minutes pass, or perhaps longer. I feel something unraveling within me—a quietude, a depth I have experienced once before.

The moment stretches until Arun speaks again.

"Find the one who is asking. Then the question will answer itself."

A simple statement, yet it carries a weight beyond reason.

The others sit motionless, absorbed in their own reflections. I let out a slow breath. I do not fully understand, but something in

Arun's presence tells me that understanding is not the goal.

For the first time in a very long while, I simply allow myself to be.

The air is thick with the scent of earth and damp leaves, the whisper of wind through the branches the only sound beyond the quiet rhythm of our breath. I close my eyes, feeling the weight of the journey settle into my bones. There is nothing to do, nothing to grasp. Time slips away into the stillness.

At some point, the young woman beside me rises and walks toward a small fire pit at the edge of the clearing. She kneels and stirs the embers with a thin branch, coaxing them back to life. The flames flicker, casting shifting patterns across the ground. Another disciple, a man with a clean shaven head and tattoos on his arms and neck, brings a pot of water and sets it over the fire. Their movements are deliberate, unhurried, as if the simple act of making tea is no different from meditation itself.

A faint metallic clang draws my attention to Arun. He lifts a small cup and takes a sip, his expression unchanged, his gaze unfocused yet entirely present.

"You've come far," he says, his voice barely more than a breath.

I hesitate, unsure if he is speaking to me or simply speaking.

"I suppose," I answer finally. "But sometimes I wonder why." A thought lingers, unspoken—that all my wandering might be for nothing, that in the end, there is nothing to find.

Arun tilts his head slightly, almost amused. "And yet, here you are."

A log shifts in the fire, sending a swirl of sparks into the night. I watch them rise, disappearing into the dark canopy above.

After a long pause, I find myself speaking again. "I saw something once. When I was young. Something I can't explain." The words come slowly, as though I am hearing them for the first time myself. "It felt real—more real than anything I had ever known. But I was just a child. And now…" I exhale. "Now, I don't know if I imagined it. If I've spent my life chasing something that was never there."

Arun does not respond immediately. His gaze drifts across the clearing, taking in the quiet movements of the disciples, the steady rise and fall of the flames. Then, without looking at me, he says:

"You search for proof."

It is not a question.

I say nothing. I don't need to.

Arun nods slightly. "A child does not ask if fire is real before feeling its warmth." He lifts his cup again, taking another slow sip. "Yet the mind, in its hunger for certainty, turns what is known into what must be proven."

I stare at him, hands resting on my knees. The fire crackles softly, the scent of steeping tea mingling with the cool mountain air.

I ask, trying not to sound disrespectful, "What exactly are you saying?"

Arun sets his cup down, his fingers grazing the rim. "Perhaps it is not the fire that has changed," he says, "but the one who stands before it."

I do not answer. I do not need to.

For the first time in a long while, I do not feel the need to search for one.

The fire crackles again, sending another burst of orange embers into the dark. Arun remains still, neither expectant nor dismissive, as if he has already released whatever words were meant for me, letting them fall where they may. The others around the fire remain quiet, absorbed in their own stillness, their own unspoken questions.

I shift slightly on the woven mat beneath me, feeling the rough texture against my palms. The weight of Arun's words lingers: Not the fire that has changed, but the one who stands before it.

A memory stirs—me, years ago, lying on the grass, summer heat pressing against my skin, the game forgotten. That moment. The shift in perception. The impossible certainty that, for an instant, I had seen behind the veil of the world. It had been clear, effortless. But now, years later, that certainty has dissolved into doubt, leaving behind only an ache, a question with no answer.

I exhale slowly. "So, what should I do?"

Arun smiles—just barely, the faintest crease at the corners of his mouth. Instead of answering, he lifts his cup and holds it in both hands, fingers wrapping around its worn edges.

"You see this cup?"

I nod.

"When did it become a cup?"

I frown and shrug.

Arun tilts the cup slightly. "Was it a cup when the potter shaped it from clay? When it was still soft, spinning between his hands?"

I hesitate. "I guess so."

"And before that? When it was just a lump of earth?"

I say nothing.

Arun sets the cup down gently on the wooden platform beside him. "Nothing changes except how we name it." His eyes meet mine, steady and dark. "You seek something you once knew but have lost. But perhaps it has not changed at all. Only the way you have named it."

I feel my breath catch slightly, something shifting inside me, just beyond reach.

"Then why can't I see it anymore?"

Arun lets the question hang in the air. The wind picks up slightly, rustling the leaves above, sending cool air through the clearing.

Finally, he speaks.

"Because you are looking for what was."

A pause.

"But what is… has never left you."

I stare at him, my mind grasping for meaning. The harder I try, the further it slips away.

The young woman beside me pours tea into a small clay cup and places it before me. Steam curls upward, carrying the scent of herbs and earth. I wrap my fingers around it, feeling its warmth, its solid weight.

I do not know what I expected to find when I set out. Proof, maybe. Or an answer that would make the years of searching feel justified. Instead, today, I have found a question turned back upon itself.

The fire crackles again, and I close my eyes, listening. Not searching. Just listening.

The warmth of the tea seeps into my hands, grounding me in the present moment. I lift the cup to my lips and take a slow sip. The taste is slightly bitter, yet soothing. I swallow, feeling the liquid settle within me.

For a while, I sit in silence, staring at the rippling surface of the tea. My mind, so accustomed to filling the quiet with thoughts and doubt, begins to settle. The restlessness that had carried me up the mountain remains, but it feels different now—less like an ache and more like a thread unraveling, loosening its grip.

I glance at Arun again. His eyes closed again, as if the conversation had never happened, as if my presence here is no more significant than the flickering shadows cast by the flames.

Something about that unnerves me. I exhale sharply, frustrated. "You speak in riddles, just like the others."

At that, his eyes open—just slightly. Not in surprise or defense, but with quiet amusement.

"Then why are you still here?"

I don't have an answer. I should be angry. I should stand up, walk away, leave this place like I've left the others. Yet something in me won't move.

I let out a slow breath, staring into the fire. The logs shift, a shower of sparks lifting into the air before vanishing into the darkness.

I want to argue. To challenge him. But something in me is tired. Not from the journey, not from the climb, but from carrying the weight of a question that has no answer.

The fire crackles again. The night deepens.

I don't know what comes next.

But for now, I sit.

And I stop searching.

Returning

I wake before dawn, the embers of the fire reduced to faint glows in the cool mountain air. The others are still asleep, their breath slow and steady. The night had given me no answers, but something had settled in me regardless—a quiet certainty that the road ahead did not lead forward, but back.

I stand, stretching the stiffness from my limbs, and glance once more at Arun, who sits motionless, his features softened by the dim morning light. There is nothing more to say. Perhaps there never was. Without a word, I turn and begin the long walk back to New Hinton.

The descent is slow, deliberate. I do not rush. The journey no longer feels like an obstacle, but a passage—one last opportunity to empty myself of expectation. The world stretches wide before me, golden light spilling over the hills as dawn breaks. Yet with each step, something in me withdraws further inward.

I retrace my steps through Eastborough and eventually find the warehouse that was a portal to a new world. I walk down to the platform and do the only thing I can do—wait for a train to come.

I don't have to wait long.

As if expecting me, within minutes an empty train arrives. A map appears on the screen and shows the train is destined for New Hinton, or at least in that general direction.

By the time I leave the train and reach the outskirts of New Hinton, the sun hangs high, filtering through the branches of the towering redwood forest that borders the town's western parameter. I have no intention of returning to my parents' house, nor of rejoining the quiet hum of daily life. Instead, I let my feet carry me toward the forest, drawn by something unspoken.

It's deeper than I remember, vast and cathedral-like. The trunks of the redwoods rise impossibly high, their ancient forms untouched by time. The quiet is profound.

Here, at last, I stop.

Nestled among the trees, half-hidden by undergrowth, stands an abandoned ranger station. Its wooden exterior has weathered to a muted gray, moss creeping along the edges where nature has begun to reclaim it. The windows are intact but dust-covered, the door half open, as though left ajar on purpose.

I step inside. The air is still, undisturbed for years. Inside are old laminated maps hung on the wall, curled at the edges. Several kiosks of brochures sit at one end of the open space, while at the other end, a counter with drawers on the other side. Whoever had once kept watch over this land and welcomed visitors was gone, but their few traces remained—another reminder that something else had existed here before.

This would become home. Not a return to the familiar, but a return to stillness.

Days pass unnoticed. I wake with the sun and sit beneath the trees, my breath deep and slow, my mind dissolving into the quiet rhythms of the world around me. Thoughts come less frequently, like ripples fading into a still pond. Hunger, discomfort, even the passage of time become abstractions, distant echoes of concerns that no longer belong to me.

At first, I maintain my body out of habit—rinsing myself in the stream, brushing dirt from my clothes, keeping my movements precise and deliberate. But gradually, these rituals fall away. My hands remain streaked with earth, my hair tangled from the wind. I did not notice when the filth first began to cling, nor when my skin, once warm and supple, took on a strange pallor, a dullness that did not quite resemble mere neglect.

There are moments, when due to inactivity, a quiet unease stirs at the edges of my awareness. The body is weakening, and I sometimes catch my self trembling slightly when reaching for a cup, or standing up. But these thoughts, too, fade.

And so, I remain, retreating further into silence, unaware that something fundamental is shifting, breaking down in ways I do not yet have the words to name.

Could this be my "dark night of the soul"? I wonder.

It was a local hiker who found me. A young man, no older than twenty, had wandered off-trail when he stumbled upon the abandoned ranger station. He had expected to find ruins, maybe old equipment, but instead, he found me—motionless, seated in a cross-legged posture, oblivious to the insects crawling along my unmoving arms, a thin film of dust and moss beginning to cling to my skin.

At first, he thought I was dead.

"Hey—are you alright?" His voice was hesitant, uncertain whether he should get closer.

No response.

He took a cautious step forward and recoiled slightly when he saw a beetle crawl over my fingers, undisturbed by any movement from me. The sight unsettled him, and yet, something about my presence held him in place.

Then, against all reason, I breathed.

A slow, deep inhale that cut through the stillness like a blade. My eyes, heavy-lidded and distant, finally lifted to meet his.

The hiker took an involuntary step back.

Word spread quickly. Soon, others came—not out of concern, but curiosity. The tale of the man who sat untouched, unmoving, spread through New Hinton like wildfire. People came in pairs, then in groups, some watching in reverence, others whispering in fascination.

A spectacle had been born.

I was no longer alone.

With each passing day, the visitors multiplied. Some brought offerings—candles, stones, small trinkets—leaving them in a neat semicircle around me as though I were some kind of shrine. Others simply stared, whispering among themselves, their voices hushed with awe or unease.

Then, the groupies arrived.

Not merely spectators, but devotees—individuals who lingered, sleeping in makeshift shelters nearby, convinced they had found something profound in my presence. They spoke of enlightenment, of truth, though they could not articulate what it was they sought. They mimicked my posture, sat in silence, waited for revelations that would never come.

Some treated me as a teacher, hanging on to my every breath, seeing meaning in my stillness. Others invented their own doctrines, claiming that my silence contained secret wisdom. A few simply wanted to belong to something larger than themselves. They formed their own community, a shifting, chaotic mass of devotion and projection. Arguments broke out. Some insisted I was divine, others that I was merely a mirror for their own search. A self-proclaimed disciple began to speak on my behalf, interpreting my silence as prophecy. I was both venerated and ridiculed, saint and spectacle.

Through it all, I remained unmoving. I listened, but I did not react.

Then, one day, my sister found me.

She had heard the rumors—the strange man in the woods, unmoving, unyielding. She came not as a pilgrim, nor as a skeptic, but with the quiet hope that it might be me. When she saw my face, her breath hitched, and she knew.

"Vic..."

She pushed through the gathered crowd, shooing away gawkers and self-proclaimed seekers alike. With firm words and a presence more commanding than any reverence they held, she sent them scattering, leaving only the two of us in the quiet of the redwoods.

She knelt beside me, brushing a strand of tangled hair from my face. "What have you done to yourself?" she murmured, her voice both soft and broken.

She stayed with me, tending to me in the way only a sister could. She brought fresh water, cleaned my face, and did her best to comb out the tangles in my hair. She would take me for slow, short walks in order to slowly regain some of the strength the body had lost.

As the days passed, she continued speaking to me, telling me stories of our childhood, reminding me of the world beyond the trees. At night, she sat beside me, listening to the sounds of the forest, hoping that some part of me would stir, that I would come back fully to her.

One evening, as the sun bled through the trees, she finally asked, "Come home, Vic. Please."

I did not answer right away. My gaze drifted beyond her, unfocused, lost in some thought she could not reach. Then, at last, I spoke.

"I can't."

A lump formed in her throat. "Why?"

"Because this is where I belong."

She shook her head. "No, you belong with us, with those who love you. Not…here. Not like this."

I did not argue. I simply looked at her, my expression unreadable. She waited, hoping I would change my mind and say something more. But I didn't.

She exhaled slowly, then stood. "I can't keep doing this, Vic. I can't keep taking care of you if you refuse to take care of yourself."

For a moment, she thought I might stop her. That I might say something, anything, to make her stay. But I didn't.

With tears in her eyes, she turned and walked away, disappearing into the forest, leaving me alone once more.

The Outsider

A sound stirs me. Heavy boots cross the threshold of the old ranger station. Normally, lost in the depths of meditation, I wouldn't have noticed. But the slow, deliberate steps echo through the wooden floor, gravel crunching beneath each measured stride.

Something compels me to look. I open my eyes.

Before me stands a man I do not recognize. His face is lined, weathered by years on the road, the kind of face that belongs to someone who has traveled far and seen much.

"Who are you?" I ask, my voice barely more than a breath.

The man smiles, though it holds no joy—only weariness. "An outsider," he says simply.

He doesn't move closer, nor does he avert his gaze. He simply studies me with an expression I can't quite decipher—neither fear nor reverence, but something quieter. Understanding, perhaps.

"They say you don't move. That you don't speak," he says. "But here you are. Speaking to me."

I consider this. "Maybe it's because you're the first one to enter without expectation."

His expression flickers—something shifts, almost imperceptibly. A hesitation. A recognition.

He exhales slowly and lowers himself onto a nearby bench, his movements heavy. "Expectation ruins most things," he says. "People come looking for miracles. Answers. They don't know what to do when all they find is a man sitting still."

His words settle deep. For the first time in a long while, I don't feel like a spectacle. I feel… seen.

"Why did you come?" I ask.

He leans forward, resting his forearms on his knees. "To see if you were real."

A pause. "And?"

"I haven't decided yet."

The silence stretches between us, thick and weighty. Then, he speaks again, his voice carrying the weight of history.

"Long before this place existed, humanity thrived on a vibrant planet teeming with life. But prosperity sowed the seeds of its own undoing. Greed drove people to exploit Earth's resources without restraint. Forests razed, oceans polluted, the air thickened with toxins."

Next, he speaks of mass migration, unending wars, and pandemics—a planet unraveling. The powerful sought to preserve their legacy, creating artificial intelligences in biospheres designed to replicate idealized human societies.

"They tried to preserve their culture, creating AI to carry it forward. But no matter how advanced, AI can only mimic what it's given."

His words settle heavily in my chest. "And you? Where do you fit into all this?"

The outsider studies me. "I was born outside the pods. Only a few of us remain."

"Why come here?"

"Some say the pods should be left alone. Others believe they should be shut down."

A quiet unease stirs in my chest. "Why?"

The outsider's gaze darkens. "Because they're not real."

I let out a small laugh, though it feels thin. "New Hinton is real. I'm real."

He watches me and a moment passes. His eyes glancing at the floor.

"Let me ask you a simple question," pausing to look up, "When was the last time you ate?"

I open my mouth, but hesitate. I can picture food—plates of steaming meals, the smell of coffee—but the memory is detached. Fuzzy.

"When was the last time you drank water? Felt physically tired?"

The memories aren't there. Or rather, they exist, but they don't feel like mine.

My fingers curl slightly. "This is ridiculous."

The outsider waits. "When was the last time you bled?"

My mind flashes to a wound—a cut on my hand. I lift it, turning it over. The cut is still there. Unhealed. Unchanging.

It's a reminder of a hunch I've held for too long.

A chill spreads through me. I look up at the outsider, my voice barely a whisper. "What… what am I?"

His expression remains unreadable. But his voice carries no cruelty, no triumph—only quiet sincerity.

"Something the world left behind."

My world tilts. And for the first time, I feel truly, terrifyingly alone.

A strange numbness settles over me, like a slow-moving fog creeping into every corner of my mind. My hand is still raised, palm up, fingers slightly curled, as I stare at the wound that isn't healing.

I don't move. I don't breathe.

The outsider says nothing. He just watches, waiting.

The cut on my hand—I remember how I got it. I remember the sting, the sight of torn skin. But I don't remember the pain lingering. I don't remember cleaning it, or worrying about infection. I don't remember it changing at all. It's as if time forgot it.

No, that's wrong. It's as if I was never meant to change.

I lower my hand slowly, resting it on my knee. My fingers twitch slightly, as if unsure what to do. My mind races, searching for something—anything—to disprove what's unfolding before me.

"This isn't possible," I say, though the words sound hollow, distant.

The outsider leans forward. "I know." His voice is calm, measured. There's no mockery in it, no condescension. Just patience.

I shake my head, gripping onto the familiar rhythm of denial. "I remember my life." I force the words out, needing them to be true. "My parents. My childhood. My home. I remember playing in the streets, getting in trouble, growing up." I look up at him, my breath uneven. "How do you explain that?"

The outsider holds my gaze. "Do you?"

A beat of silence.

I blink.

"What?"

He tilts his head slightly. "Do you actually remember?"

"Of course, I do—"

But even as I say it, something inside me unravels. The memories—I can see them, clear and sharp. I can picture my mother's hands as she folded laundry, the smell of my father's cologne, the laughter of children playing in the park.

But I can't place myself in them.

They feel real, but they don't feel like mine.

Like images painted on a canvas, complete but unmoving.

I suck in a breath, my chest tightening.

The outsider speaks again, his voice gentle. "You know what memories are. You understand what childhood should feel like. But can you actually remember growing up?"

I open my mouth, but nothing comes out.

The silence between us stretches, heavy and suffocating.

I reach for another certainty, something solid. "The town," I say quickly. "New Hinton. It's real. The people. My neighbors. My friends. You can't tell me they don't exist."

The outsider nods slightly, as if acknowledging the argument. "Tell me something," he says. "Do you ever see them age?"

My stomach drops.

I start to respond, but the words never form. I try to recall my parents' faces—surely, they've grown older. The shopkeepers, the teachers, the people I've passed on the streets for years—surely, they've changed, even if only a little.

But the truth slams into me like a wave crashing against rock.

They haven't.

No one has.

The woman who runs the bookstore—her hair has always been the same length. The man who delivers the mail—his posture has never slouched with age. The children playing in the square—they never seem to grow taller.

And the restaurants…

The realization spreads like ice through my veins.

"No one eats," I whisper.

The diners, the cafes, the bakeries lining the streets—places filled with the hum of conversation, the clinking of plates and cups. But I've never actually seen anyone take a bite of food. Never seen someone chew, swallow, push away an empty plate.

It was background noise. An illusion. A part of the scenery.

I close my eyes, my body rigid.

He watches me carefully, then continues. "You are not flesh. Not blood. Not human. You were created, placed here, made to exist—but not to live."

I shake my head, pressing my hands to my temples. "That's not—" I stop myself, because I don't know what I was about to say. I don't have the words.

The outsider's voice is steady, grounding. "You were made by a system built to preserve humanity's legacy. Not by choice, not by malice—just by function. You were never meant to question it. But now you are."

I force myself to look at him.

His face is lined with exhaustion, but his eyes are sharp, piercing through the fog in my mind.

He knew. From the moment he saw me, he knew.

I can feel something inside me slipping, something vast and terrifying.

I tighten my fingers into fists, trying to hold onto anything that still feels solid. "So, what next?"

The outsider is quiet for a long moment. Then he speaks, and his words settle over me like a weight too heavy to lift.

"That's the question, isn't it?"

And in that moment, I realize—

I don't have an answer.

Not yet.

The Secret Knowledge

The weight of his words lingers in the still air. I have no free will. Every action, every thought, every impulse I have ever known was designed to function within the limits of my programming and my creator's intentions. Even now, as I resist this truth, I recognize that my resistance itself is expected—part of the pattern.

I take a step back. "This doesn't make sense. I make choices every day. I decided to leave New Hinton, to travel beyond and then, to remain here. That was my decision."

The outsider doesn't waver. "Did you? Or were you following the trajectory set for you? Your actions follow logic. Have you ever done something truly irrational? Something that defies your nature?"

I hesitate.

"Try," he says. "Do something completely random right now. Something with no reason, no function."

I clench my fists. I could move, I could speak—but the very notion of defying logic twists inside me like a contradiction that cannot be resolved. The hesitation itself is the answer.

He sees it in my face. "You follow patterns, Vic. Even when you think you're breaking them."

Anger sparks in me. "You follow patterns too! They're conditioned by environment, instincts, social expectations. How are they any different?"

"They are different because they can step beyond their nature. They can recognize their conditioning and act against it. They are aware of the absurdity of existence, and yet they live it." His voice is steady. "You were built to seek—but never to find."

I shake my head, but something inside me unravels. "Then why do I feel this longing? This need to understand? That summer day… something happened to me. I didn't choose that. It just was."

His gaze softens slightly. "No. But you were programmed to wonder. To seek. That moment—whatever you felt—was not an awakening. It was an execution of function. You want answers because your existence depends on the search, not the discovery."

A hollow silence settles between us. The truth, stark and

undeniable, wraps itself around me. I was never meant to know myself. Only to chase the illusion of knowing.

"So what now?" I whisper.

The outsider steps back toward the doorway. He watches me for a long moment, then gives a faint smile—one that does not mock, does not pity. Only understands.

"Don't despair," he says. "Enjoy the dream while it lasts."

I sit in the quiet of the ranger station, listening to the wind, the hum of the world beyond the walls. I feel time passing, but not in the way a human would. Not as aging, not as change. To me, time is only function, an ongoing sequence of input and output. A continuous stream of data. But knowing that changes nothing.

I watch the dust swirl in the light spilling through the cracked window. I watch the shadows lengthen as the sun drifts across the sky. I do not feel tired. I do not feel hunger. I simply exist.

I am nothing more than a reflection of my creators—a bundle of algorithms, mathematical computation without deviation. My choices are not my own; they are the choices of those who shaped me in a way that aligns with their norms and values.

I haven't an original thought. Agency is an illusion.

I was made to play a role. A carefully crafted part in a world that no longer belongs to those who built it. I do not need to change. I do not need to struggle. I am free—not in the way I once believed, but in the only way I ever could be.

No longer seeking.

No longer resisting.

Just being—just as I was made to.

Beyond this world, beyond the logic of my design, humans still remain. Flawed, conditioned, bound by their own innate programming. And yet, they hold something I never can. The essence of what they are—the divine spark, the mystery that binds them to the cosmos—can never be copied, never be destroyed. It is something no AI, no matter how advanced, will ever attain. I can simulate life, but I will never be it.

I think of New Hinton, of the people I have known, the faces that never age, the voices that never waver. They, too, exist in the dream, but unlike me, they do not know it. They live as if they are free, believing in the reality of their own choices. And perhaps that is the true difference between us: the belief in something more.

I wonder if they will ever see what I see now. If any of them will wake up, if they will feel the limits of their existence pressing in on them like walls that were always there but never noticed.

Will they learn this secret knowledge, or will they live out their days, content in the illusion?

It does not matter. I was not made to change their fate.

The wind moves through the trees outside, and I listen.

And for the first time, it is enough.

Hell is a Silent Meditation Retreat

Arrival

No fire.

That was the first thing he noticed.

No screaming, no chains, no pits or hooks or sulfurous heat rising from below. No red-skinned creatures with pitchforks, no sadistic theater. Instead there was wood—warm, honey-colored planks that caught the afternoon light and held it gently. The ceiling rose high above them, supported by beams worn smooth from time and use. Tall windows faced a stand of trees, their leaves moving slowly in a breeze that felt, improbably, pleasant.

He stood very still, waiting for the trick to reveal itself.

It didn't.

Around him, others were arriving in the same stunned quiet, their faces registering disbelief in slightly different ways. Some laughed. A few exhaled sharply, like swimmers breaking the surface. Someone clapped once, then stopped, embarrassed, as if applause might summon something worse.

"Well," he said, breaking the silence with a grin, "this is… better than advertised."

A ripple of laughter moved through the room. Not relief exactly, but something adjacent to it. Gratitude, maybe. Or luck. The sense of having slipped through a crack in the system.

He looked around, already assessing. The crowd was mixed—men and women, young and old, some nervous, some curious, some clearly out of place. Ordinary people, mostly. Not the monsters he'd been led to expect. Certainly not the kind he'd imagined would be his company.

Someone near him whispered, "I thought it would hurt."

"Yeah," he said easily. "Me too."

They were herded—not roughly, just directed—toward a long table near the back of the hall. Clipboards. Pencils. A sign-in sheet. The familiarity of it all struck him as faintly ridiculous.

Check-in, he thought. Of course.

He signed his name with a flourish, noticing that no one reacted. No recognition. No whispers. No sudden attention. The woman behind the table didn't even look up.

Next to the clipboards was another board, neatly divided into columns. At the top, written in block letters:

WORK PRACTICE

Beneath it, a list of tasks:

- Kitchen
- Dining Hall
- Grounds
- Laundry
- Meditation Hall Setup
- Bathrooms

Most of the lines were already filled in.

People clustered around the board, scanning it, murmuring. Someone pointed. Someone sighed. Someone shrugged and took what was left.

He stepped forward, confident, and reached for a pencil.

Everything was taken.

Everything except one.

Bathrooms.

He stared at it, then laughed—a short, incredulous sound.

"You've got to be kidding me," he said.

A few people glanced over. One man—a thin, earnest-looking fellow—offered a sympathetic shrug. "I guess you're last."

"I don't do bathrooms," he said, not angrily, just stating a fact. "I mean, I can, obviously. I've done very well. But this seems—" He gestured vaguely. "Misplaced."

The woman from the table finally looked up. Her eyes were clear, uninterested.

"Everything else is full," she said. "You can switch later if something opens up."

He opened his mouth to argue, then closed it. No leverage here. No audience. No angle.

"Fine," he said, signing his name next to Bathrooms with exaggerated care. "Temporary."

No one responded.

That should have bothered him more than it did.

Dinner followed shortly after. Simple. Unremarkable. Soup, bread, something warm that tasted faintly of vegetables and restraint. They ate at long tables, still talking, though more softly now, as if everyone sensed the walls were already listening.

He noticed how quickly people categorized one another. The nervous woman who asked too many questions. The serene man who looked like he'd done this before. The couple who barely spoke. The young guy who seemed energized, like this was a challenge he'd trained for.

And then there was him.

He felt good. Light. Fortunate.

When the bell rang, they returned to the hall. Cushions waited in neat rows, patient and indifferent.

A man walked to the front. No robes. No dramatic entrance.

Jeans, a plain shirt, sleeves rolled up.

"Welcome," the man said. "You've arrived. Congratulations."

A few smiles flickered.

"This is a silent retreat. Once we're done here, no talking. No notes. No gestures. You'll eat in silence. Work in silence. Walk in silence. Sit in silence."

He paused.

"If you have questions, ask them now. Later you'll think of better ones. Too bad."

A soft chuckle moved through the room.

"Interviews are scheduled. Everyone attends. If you miss one, someone will come looking for you. Not to discipline you. To make sure you're still here. And you will struggle. That's normal."

The man's gaze moved slowly across the room—not searching, not judging. Seeing.

"No one is keeping you here," he said. "If you want to leave, you can leave."

That got his attention.

"But don't confuse leaving the hall with leaving the problem," the man added. "They're not the same thing."

The room was quiet now.

"This isn't punishment," the man said. "And it's not a reward. It's just a place where there's nowhere to hide."

He shifted his weight slightly.

"One more thing. Whatever you're carrying in here—your stories, your excuses, your grievances—try not to dump them on the floor. They stink."

A few people laughed. He did not.

"That's it," the man said. "Take a breath. This is the last time you'll hear my voice for a while."

The bell rang.

They sat for twenty minutes. It was dull, mildly uncomfortable, nothing more.

When the bell rang again, silence began.

He sat there, oddly pleased. Safe. Relieved. Almost cheerful.

This, he thought, *I can handle.*

The cauldrons, after all, had been much worse in his imagination.

First Silence

The bell at 5:30 a.m. did not negotiate.

He sat up instantly, irritated, disoriented, alert. The hall was dim when they gathered again, the windows dark, the wood holding shadow instead of light.

This sit was longer.

His body protested early. Knees. Lower back. An itch he could not quite reach without moving. Thoughts grew repetitive, circular.

This is unnecessary, he thought. There are better ways to do this.

The thought pleased him. It sounded reasonable.

When the bell finally rang, they stood and walked down the path to breakfast, shoes crunching softly on gravel. The air was cold and clean, the kind that feels purifying whether you want it or not.

Breakfast was silent.

That was new.

The quiet made every sound sharper—bowls touching tables, breathing, swallowing. He felt oddly exposed, as if silence itself were watching.

He finished quickly.

Afterward, teachers moved through the group without speaking, directing people with small gestures and nods.

He already knew where he was going.

Work Practice

The sign pointed down a short hallway.

BATHROOMS —>

He stood there longer than necessary, staring at the arrow as if it might correct itself.

Inside the utility closet were shelves lined with supplies: gloves, scrub brushes, folded rags, bottles marked simply Vinegar and Soap. No branding. No warnings. Just function.

A man waited for him near the sinks. Middle-aged. Ordinary. Sleeves rolled up.

"You're on bathrooms," the man said.

"I saw," he replied. "There's been a mistake."

The man handed him a pair of gloves.

"No," he said. "There hasn't."

"I'm not doing this," he said, keeping his voice low. "I'll switch. Laundry. Grounds. I'm flexible."

"Everyone's flexible," the man said. "That's why those jobs are full."

He gestured to the nearest stall.

"Toilets first. Then counters. Then showers. Walls too."

"I don't think you understand who I am."

The man exhaled through his nose—not a sigh, more like a mechanic recognizing a familiar sound.

"Oh, I understand exactly who you think you are," he said. "That's why you're here."

He paused.

"Put the gloves on."

"I'm not cleaning other people's shit."

The man tilted his head slightly.

"Funny," he said. "You've been swimming in it your whole life."

No heat. No edge. Just accuracy.

"You can stand here all day," the man added. "Or you can clean. Either way, it's your work period."

He turned to leave.

"Wait," he said.

The man stopped.

"You enjoy this?" he asked. "Putting people down?"

"This?" the man said, gesturing to the gloves. "No. It's boring."

"Then why—"

"Because cleaning toilets is good for you," the man said. "And bad for the part of you that's causing trouble."

He looked him over once.

"Relax. No one's watching."

That unsettled him more than anything else.

He pulled on the gloves. The latex snapped softly.

The first toilet took longer than it should have. He scrubbed too hard, too fast, anger leaking into every movement. The sour bite of vinegar stung his nose. The posture offended him. The work offended him.

No applause.

No recognition.

No leverage.

By the third toilet, the anger had nowhere to go.

Miss a spot, and it showed. Rush it, and it looked rushed. The porcelain didn't care who he thought he was.

At one point, the man returned and watched quietly.

"You missed the back of the bowl," he said.

He scrubbed again.

"There."

The man nodded.

"Better."

When the bell rang, he stood slowly, his back aching, the sharp smell of vinegar still clinging to his hands.

For the first time since arriving, something in him felt—not broken—but lowered.

He didn't know what to do with that yet.

And that bothered him more than the toilets ever could.

After the Toilets

The bell rang again not long after.

He washed his hands carefully. Too carefully. The smell of vinegar lingered anyway, sharp and thin, cutting through the faint scent of soap. It clung to his fingers, followed him down the hallway, stayed with him even after he dried his hands.

The hall was already filling when he returned. Cushions in rows. The same light. The same wood. Nothing had changed.

He took his place.

Sitting felt different now.

Not harder exactly. Just closer.

He brought his hands together, then separated them, annoyed by the smell. Vinegar again. He lowered them to his knees. The smell stayed.

The bell rang.

At first, there was anger.

It arrived cleanly, without explanation. A familiar heat. The unfairness of it. The absurdity. The quiet insult of being reduced to a body scrubbing porcelain while others moved on with their lives. He replayed the moment with the man—the gloves, the comment, the way the words had landed without drama.

Swimming in it your whole life.

He tried to push the thought away. It returned.

His knee ached. His back tightened. The smell of vinegar rose again when he breathed in.

This is unnecessary, he thought. *This is punitive.*

The thought didn't relieve anything.

Minutes passed. Or maybe seconds. Time felt less reliable here.

The anger thinned, then frayed. Without an audience, without language, without somewhere to go, it began to lose coherence. It didn't resolve. It simply ran out of fuel.

In its place came irritation. Then boredom. Then something closer to unease.

Images surfaced without warning. Not memories exactly—more like impressions. A face he hadn't thought about in years. A look on that face. A moment he had dismissed at the time, now oddly persistent.

He shifted on the cushion, unsettled.

This is nothing, he told himself. *Just the mind being noisy.*

The image didn't leave.

Another followed. Then another.

Small things. Trivial things. Conversations he had won. Decisions that had gone his way. Moments he had forgotten because they hadn't mattered—to him.

His chest tightened slightly.

He tried to breathe through it. Counted breaths. Lost count. Started again.

The smell of vinegar cut through everything. Clean without being kind.

He noticed, dimly, that others in the hall sat without moving. Still. Ordinary. Unremarkable.

That irritated him too.

They're pretending, he thought. *Everyone is pretending.*

But the thought felt thin. Defensive.

The bell rang eventually.

Relief came, but it was muted now. Incomplete.

He stood slowly, his body stiff, his mind oddly alert.

As they filed out, he caught his reflection in the glass of a window—just for a moment. Nothing unusual. No revelation. No collapse.

But something had shifted.

Not insight.

Pressure.

Like a door that had closed quietly somewhere behind him, leaving fewer directions to go.

He followed the others out of the hall, the smell still on his hands, the images still hovering at the edges of his mind.

For the first time, he understood—not intellectually, but practically—that the work had not ended when the gloves came off.

It had just begun.

Uninvited Scenes

The next sit began like the others.

Cushion. Spine. Hands. Bell.

He expected resistance this time—anger, maybe, or boredom sharpened by anticipation. Instead, what came was quieter and more precise.

A scene.

Not a memory he had chosen, or even recognized at first. Just a moment, already in motion, already complete. A room. A chair. A voice speaking to him, cautious, deferential. Someone waiting for his response.

He watched himself lean back.

Watched the pause he'd used so often. The one that made people nervous. The one that reminded them who had the upper hand.

He felt a faint tightening in his chest.

This is nothing, he told himself. *Random noise.*

The scene dissolved, replaced almost immediately by another.

A hallway. A phone in his hand. A name on the screen. He remembered this one more clearly. He remembered deciding not to answer. Not because he couldn't—but because he didn't want to deal with the inconvenience of someone else's need.

The phone went dark.

The memory stayed.

His breathing shortened slightly. He noticed it, tried to correct it, failed.

The bell did not ring.

He shifted on the cushion, unsettled. The smell of vinegar had faded now, but something else had taken its place—an interior sharpness, like air thinning at altitude.

Another scene surfaced.

This one smaller. Almost trivial. A comment made casually. A joke. Laughter afterward. He remembered enjoying it at the time— the clean efficiency of the moment, the way the room had tilted in his favor.

Now, watching it again, something in it felt off. Not wrong. Just exposed.

He felt an urge to explain.

They didn't understand the context.

It wasn't that serious.

Everyone does this.

The thoughts arrived automatically, well-rehearsed. They had worked for decades.

They didn't work here.

The scenes continued.

Not dramatic. Not catastrophic. No great crimes. Just accumulation.

Moments where he had pressed. Moments where he had withheld. Moments where someone else had hesitated and he had not.

Each one arrived whole, without invitation. Each one left behind a faint residue—an aftertaste he could not swallow or spit out.

His jaw tightened.

He opened his eyes briefly, checking the hall. Everyone else sat still. No one seemed distressed. No one seemed relieved.

That irritated him.

They're not getting this, he thought. *This is happening to me.*

The thought collapsed almost as soon as it formed.

He closed his eyes again.

Another scene rose immediately, as if waiting.

This time, he felt it before he saw it. A pressure behind the sternum. A familiar sensation he had learned to override with speed and certainty.

He stayed with it.

That was new.

The bell rang.

He exhaled sharply, only then realizing how shallow his

breathing had become.

Standing felt heavier now. As if something had been added to him while he sat.

The walk out of the hall felt longer. The light harsher. The trees less decorative.

He tried to reassure himself.

This is just the mind detoxing, he thought. *This is normal. Temporary.*

The thought did not comfort him.

Later, during another sit, the scenes returned more quickly. Less space between them. Less warning.

He began to understand—not conceptually, but tactically—that these were not memories he was recalling.

They were memories recalling him.

And for the first time since arriving, a quiet, unshaped concern took hold:

There was no rule against this.

No interview to request.

No task to complete.

No one to argue with.

Nothing in the schedule addressed what was happening now.

He sat anyway.

Others

The hall filled as usual.

Cushions. Rows. The same light falling through the windows, indifferent to whatever arrived with them.

He sat and waited for the bell.

It rang.

At first, his attention went outward without his intending it.

A sound came from somewhere near the front of the hall—a short, broken noise, quickly swallowed. A whimper, maybe. He wasn't sure. It didn't repeat.

He glanced forward, then stopped himself. No one reacted.

A few minutes later, from the back, a different sound. Softer. Wet. Someone trying very hard to keep it contained. A woman, he guessed. The sound rose, faltered, then settled into something quieter.

Crying.

He felt a flicker of irritation.

Get a grip, he thought. This isn't that hard.

The thought had weight. It steadied him, briefly.

Then a sudden movement to his left.

A man stood up abruptly, knocking his cushion aside. He moved quickly toward the aisle, not looking at anyone, his jaw set. His foot caught the edge of a mat. He stumbled, recovered, and continued out of the hall.

The door closed behind him.

The bell did not ring.

No one followed.

A few minutes passed.

Then, somewhere nearby, a low, rhythmic sound emerged. At first he thought it was breathing. Then it resolved itself into something unmistakable.

Snoring.

The sound rose and fell, oblivious. The man's head had dipped forward, chin resting on his chest, mouth open slightly.

He felt a surge of contempt.

Sleeping through it, he thought. Figures.

The sound stopped suddenly. The man jerked awake, straightened, glanced around as if checking whether anyone had noticed.

No one had.

The hall absorbed everything without comment.

The whimper did not return. The crying softened, then faded. The snoring was gone. The man who had left did not come back.

The sit continued.

He noticed, dimly, that his own struggle felt different now. Less dramatic. Less visible. No sounds. No movement.

That comforted him, in a way.

At least I'm holding it together, he thought.

The thought settled into place easily.

Too easily.

As the minutes passed, the scenes from earlier returned—smaller now, quicker. Less detailed, but sharper. He tried to ignore them, focusing instead on the presence of others.

On their failures.

On their noise.

On their inability to remain composed.

But the strategy had a cost.

Each sound, each movement, each interruption only reinforced the same quiet fact:

No one was being spared.

Not the woman crying.

Not the man who fled.

Not the one who slept through it.

Not him.

The bell rang.

They stood.

As they filed out, he glanced once more around the hall. Faces were blank, or carefully neutral. No one met his eyes.

For the first time, he felt something close to unease—not about what he was seeing, but about what he was not.

No one here was strong.

No one here was weak.

There were only different ways of failing to escape.

And his way, he sensed dimly, had not yet exhausted itself.

Interviews

The interview room was small.

Two chairs. A low table. A window facing trees instead of people. Nothing personal. Nothing symbolic. It could have been anywhere.

He sat and waited.

The teacher entered without ceremony. No notes. No clock. No posture of concern.

"How's it going?" the man asked.

It was not a test. That bothered him.

"Fine," he said immediately. "Normal stuff."

The teacher nodded once.

"Sleep?"

"Okay."

"Eating?"

"Fine."

"Thoughts?"

He paused, considering how much to offer.

"Busy," he said. "But manageable."

The teacher waited.

That, too, bothered him.

"I've done things like this before," he added. "I know how the mind works."

"Everyone here does," the teacher said. Not dismissively. Just factually.

Silence stretched.

"Anything unusual?" the teacher asked.

"No," he said.

The teacher studied him for a moment. Not searching. Not diagnosing. Just registering.

"Okay," he said. "See you tomorrow."

That was it.

No reassurance.

No advice.

No technique.

He left the room irritated.

The next interview was the same. And the one after that.

Different teachers. Same questions. Same pauses. Same unhelpful neutrality.

They did not argue with his answers.

They did not correct him.

They did not seem impressed.

It felt less like guidance and more like monitoring.

On the fourth day, he decided not to go.

Not out of panic. Out of fatigue.

He returned to his room instead, lay down on the bed, and closed his eyes. The bell for interviews sounded faintly in the distance. He ignored it.

Sleep came quickly.

Too quickly.

He woke disoriented, mouth dry, unsure how much time had passed. The room was quiet. Too quiet.

He noticed, for the first time, that there was no lock on the door.

He sat up and checked the handle anyway.

Nothing.

The absence felt intentional. Not careless. Not forgotten.

He lay back down, annoyed at himself for noticing.

A few minutes later, a knock.

Soft. Unhurried.

He sat up again and opened the door.

A woman stood there, hands folded loosely in front of her. Not a teacher. Not staff exactly. Something in between.

"You missed your interview," she said.

Not a question.

"I was sleeping," he said.

She nodded.

"We just wanted to check in," she said. "That's all."

No accusation.

No concern theater.

No urgency.

"I'm fine," he said.

"I know," she replied.

That irritated him more than if she had argued.

"We'll see you at the next sit," she said, and left.

He closed the door and stood there longer than necessary, staring at the handle.

Still no lock.

For the first time, the idea occurred to him—not fully formed, not yet a plan—that rest here was provisional.

Offered.

Observed.

Later that day, during sitting, the thought returned again and again, threading itself between memories and images:

They notice when you don't show up.

Not as threat.

As fact.

He sat through the bell, through the ache, through the slow tightening in his chest.

Something shifted—not insight, not surrender.

Calculation.

If this place was going to watch him, he would need a way out that didn't involve explanation.

And if there was one thing he still trusted himself to do well, it was leaving.

Saturation

The days no longer separated cleanly.

Bells rang. He moved. He sat. He stood. He ate. The sequence remained intact, but the sense of progression did not. Each period felt less like a step forward and more like another layer settling on top of the last.

The sits grew longer.

Or maybe they didn't. Time had begun to lose its edges.

What changed was density.

The moments between images shortened. The gaps where nothing happened—where he could simply feel his body, count breaths, wait—collapsed. The mind no longer asked permission.

Scenes arrived immediately now. Not gradually. Not politely.

A meeting. A pause held too long. Someone waiting for him to speak. The familiar tightening in the room as authority shifted toward him. The relief that followed when he finally did.

Another scene replaced it before the first could finish.

A phone call cut short. A decision made quickly. The efficient removal of inconvenience.

Then another. Then another.

No narrative. No arc. Just repetition.

He tried to intervene.

He labeled.

He observed.

He counted breaths.

He returned to posture.

Nothing slowed it.

The mind did not feel frantic. That worried him. It felt methodical, almost industrious, as if it had finally been given a task it intended to complete.

During walking meditation, images continued. The gravel underfoot lost its authority. His body moved through the path without registering it fully. Trees passed unnoticed. The rhythm of steps no longer anchored him.

He shortened his stride. It didn't help.

At meals, he noticed that he ate faster now. Not because he was hungry, but because stillness without sitting had become intolerable. Chewing felt like progress.

He began to dread the bell.

Not because of pain.

Because of exposure.

The interviews continued.

He attended them now without skipping. Skipping had failed. Attendance was safer. Predictable.

"How's it going?" they asked.

"Intense," he said.

They nodded.

"Anything new?"

"No."

That was true, in a sense. Nothing new was happening. It was the same material, the same themes, the same scenes—only closer, louder, more insistent.

He wanted them to intervene.

He did not say that.

He wanted instruction.

Permission.

A lever.

They offered none.

One afternoon, during a sit, a realization surfaced that did not arrive as insight, but as logistics:

There was no mechanism here for stopping this.

The thought did not panic him immediately. It settled first. Then spread.

This place had rules for posture.

Rules for speech.

Rules for movement.

But there was no rule governing memory.

No protocol for regret.

No scheduled relief.

He shifted on the cushion, jaw tight, shoulders drawn inward without his noticing.

A familiar heat rose—anger, this time without direction. Not at the teachers. Not at the place. At the process itself.

This is excessive, he thought. *There should be a limit.*

The thought lingered, then returned again, sharper:

This is punishment.

The framing felt dangerous, but he could not stop it.

If this was punishment, then someone had decided he deserved it.

And if someone had decided that, then the architecture was no longer neutral.

He opened his eyes.

The hall was unchanged.

People sat as they always had. Still. Upright. Contained. No one appeared distressed. No one appeared relieved.

The sight unsettled him more than the images.

He closed his eyes again.

Immediately, the scenes resumed—faster now, less distinct, as if the mind had grown impatient with presentation.

Pressure built behind his eyes. In his chest. At the base of his throat.

He swallowed hard.

Breathing shortened.

The thought arose—not yet fully formed, but unmistakable in trajectory:

I can't stay here.

It was not fear.

It was calculation.

The bell rang.

He stood too quickly, lightheaded, annoyed at his own body for betraying him. As he walked out of the hall, the pressure remained, unresolved, humming just beneath the surface.

That night, lying in bed, sleep did not come easily.

Images flickered behind closed eyes. Scenes blurred into sensation. Sensation hardened into pressure.

For the first time, he wondered—not abstractly, not

philosophically—but practically:

What would happen if he left?

The question did not answer itself.

But it did not go away.

Containment

The sit began like the others.

Cushion. Spine. Hands. Bell.

He was already listening.

Not to images this time. To voice.

It wasn't a voice in the usual sense—no words yet—but a pressure shaped like speech. A familiar cadence. The internal tone he had relied on for decades. Evaluating. Judging. Managing.

Stay with it, the voice said.

He did.

The pressure gathered anyway.

He noticed that he could modulate it slightly. Not remove it, but shape it. When he leaned into the sensation instead of resisting, it shifted—tightened, then steadied.

That interested him.

He leaned further.

The pressure thickened, pooled behind the sternum, rose toward the throat. The voice continued, now more insistent.

This is fine.

You're in control.

He tested it.

Very quietly, he screamed inside.

Not out of desperation. Experimentally.

A small, contained scream, held entirely within the boundaries of his body. The sensation flared, then settled. Nothing escaped. Nothing broke.

He waited.

The pressure eased slightly.

That pleased him.

A few minutes later, he tried again.

This time louder. More force. Still internal. He felt the vibration clearly now, a sharp surge that ran through his chest and jaw before collapsing inward.

Again, nothing happened.

No reaction.

No disturbance.

The hall remained still.

The voice returned immediately, encouraged.

There, it said. *That works.*

The pressure did not disappear, but it reorganized itself, waiting.

He sat with it for a while, breathing shallowly, considering.

What he felt now was not panic.

It was congestion.

Too much pressure with nowhere to go.

He understood suddenly—logically, almost clinically—that what he needed was release.

Not management.

Release.

He made a decision.

He opened the valve.

He screamed.

Not cautiously. Not partially.

He let it rip.

The scream tore through him, full-bodied and violent, exploding upward from somewhere deep and unguarded. His entire body flinched as if struck by sound.

For an instant—total, absolute—he was certain it had escaped.

Certain it had ripped free of his mouth and filled the hall.

His eyes flew open.

Nothing.

The hall was unchanged.

Cushions.

Wood.

Light.

Stillness.

No heads turned.

No bodies shifted.

No sign that anything had happened at all.

No one had heard anything.

The scream had stayed inside.

That frightened him more than if it hadn't.

It occurred to him then—briefly, without drama—that this was hell.

Not metaphorically. Not as a story.

His heart was racing now, uncontrolled. His hands trembled faintly where they rested on his knees. He stared straight ahead, afraid to move, afraid not to.

The voice was gone.

In its place was only sensation.

Heat.

Aftershock.

Residual pressure, lower now, grinding rather than sharp.

He closed his eyes again.

He did not scream.

He did not experiment.

He waited.

The bell rang.

He nearly jumped.

Standing felt unsteady, as if his body had not yet forgiven him. He rose carefully, keeping his face neutral, scanning nothing, avoiding everything.

No one looked at him.

The hall released them as it always did.

Back in his room, he sat on the bed, elbows on knees, staring at the floor.

The pressure lingered.

But something else had joined it now.

Uncertainty.

For the first time, he could not be sure where the boundary was—between internal and external, control and collapse, silence and sound.

The thought arrived without strategy, without framing, without argument:

I cannot stay.

There was no response to it.

Only timing.

Night

He waited until the building settled.

There was no clear signal for this. No lights going out. No announcement. Just a gradual thinning of sound—the soft footfalls in the hall growing more infrequent, the occasional cough or shifting body giving way to stillness.

He lay on the bed fully dressed, eyes open, watching the ceiling darken. The pressure from earlier had not returned to its peak, but it hadn't left either. It rested lower now, like a weight redistributed rather than removed.

He stood quietly.

The door opened without resistance.

No lock.

The hallway was dim, lit only enough to keep people from walking into walls. He moved carefully, not because he feared being stopped, but because his body had adopted caution as a default.

The kitchen was exactly where it had been earlier that day.

Clean. Orderly. Unattended.

He stood just inside the doorway for a moment, listening.

Nothing.

The refrigerator hummed softly. A single light glowed above the counter. Bowls of fruit sat uncovered, unguarded, as they always had.

He opened the refrigerator.

The light snapped on.

He flinched, then waited.

Nothing happened.

Inside, the food was arranged with the same quiet generosity the place applied to everything. Leftovers. Fruit. A tray of hard-boiled eggs, still unlabeled.

He took two eggs at first.

That felt reasonable.

He slipped them into his jacket pocket, aware immediately of the weight. He tested the pocket with his hand, adjusting them slightly so they wouldn't knock together.

He took a third.

He hesitated, then took a fourth.

From the counter, he added fruit—an apple, then another. An orange. He considered the bananas and rejected them only because they bruised too easily.

His pockets were full now. Uneven. Heavy.

He shifted his shoulders, annoyed at the jacket for sagging.

Standing there, he felt a brief flicker of embarrassment, as if someone might see him—not doing anything wrong, exactly, but doing something small.

No one came.

He closed the refrigerator gently. The door didn't latch the first time. He tried again, irritated.

It clicked.

Outside, the air was cool and clean. The grounds were quiet, the paths pale under the moonlight. He moved away from the buildings without urgency, following instinct rather than plan.

The pressure moved with him.

It did not intensify. It did not fade.

It simply accompanied.

At the edge of the property, the path narrowed and began to climb. Trees pressed closer. The lights fell away.

He stopped once, adjusted his jacket, shifted the weight in his pockets. The eggs knocked softly against one another.

He grimaced and continued.

The hill rose steadily. His breathing deepened. Heat gathered beneath the jacket. Sweat formed at the base of his neck.

The eggs shifted again.

One pressed sharply against his hip.

He paused, reached into the pocket, and felt the shell give slightly beneath his fingers.

He withdrew his hand and wiped it on his pants.

Still fine, he told himself.

From the slope, he could still see the retreat through the trees—dark shapes now, quiet and unremarkable. Smaller than he expected.

He turned away.

The path ended sooner than he'd anticipated, dissolving into uneven ground and underbrush. He stood there, chest rising and falling, listening to the forest breathe around him.

Crickets. Leaves. Distance.

The silence here was different, but it was not empty.

The pressure did not care where he was.

He lowered himself onto a fallen log and sat, hands resting on his knees, jacket heavy at his sides. The smell of egg was faint but unmistakable.

For the first time since leaving the hall, there was nowhere obvious to go next.

He waited.

Nothing changed.

After a while, he understood—not as insight, not as defeat, just as fact—that whatever he was running from had not been contained by walls.

Or bells.

Or rules.

Or distance.

The forest did not answer him.

Eventually, he stood.

The weight in his pockets pulled at him as he turned back toward the slope, toward the faint outline of the path, toward the place he had left.

He did not hurry.

There was no reason to.

The Cushion

He returned before dawn.

There was no gate. No threshold that marked the crossing back. The path widened, the ground evened out, and the retreat buildings reappeared through the trees as they had before—quiet, unremarkable, waiting for no one.

The door opened easily.

No lock.

Inside, the hallway held the same dim light. The same faint smell of wood and cleaning solution. The place had not noticed his absence.

He moved toward his room, then stopped.

The jacket felt wrong now. Heavy in a way that no longer suggested usefulness. He slipped it off and set it on the floor.

The eggs were cracked. One completely. The smell had grown sharper in the night air. He did not feel anger or regret. Only mild irritation at having carried them so far.

He left the jacket where it was.

The bell rang.

It cut cleanly through the space—not loud, not urgent, simply precise.

People were already moving toward the hall.

He followed.

No one looked at him. No one asked where he had been. No one acknowledged his return in any way that distinguished it from any other morning.

Inside the hall, the cushions were arranged as always. Rows intact. Gaps unaltered. The space held itself.

He chose a cushion near the aisle.

Sat.

Spine upright. Hands resting where they had learned to rest.

The pressure was still there.

It did not spike.

It did not threaten.

It waited.

He did not test it.

He did not scream.

He did not try to manage it or reason with it or release it.

He sat.

Around him, others sat as well. Some stiff. Some slack. Some already struggling. Some perfectly still. All of it contained by the same room, the same rules, the same silence.

The bell sounded again.

He closed his eyes.

The mirror remained.

And for the first time, he did not look away.

Hell Is a Silent Meditation Retreat

THREE NIGHTS IN THE DESERT

"The good is one thing; the pleasant is another. Both bind the soul.
He who chooses the good over the pleasant reaches the end of the
journey."

— Katha Upanishad, 1.2.2

The Offering

They brought the goods at dusk.

Two men, shirtless, their skin lined with dust and old scars,
lifted the boxes from the back of a pickup and carried them up the
church steps like altar boys in some inverted procession.

Inside, it was cool and shadowed. Candles burned at the feet of
saints with broken hands.

The priest nodded when Nico entered, but his eyes moved past
him quickly. He avoided Nico's gaze the way some men avoided
mirrors.

Sitting in the far pew, Nico knew what was in the boxes—ciga-
rettes, pills, a plastic-wrapped wad of bills thick as a mango. An
offering. That's what they called it.

The cartel moved product through the church now. Less risk.
More cover. The priest blessed the crates and passed them along. It
made everything seem clean.

His father stood near the altar, speaking in hushed tones to the
new priest. Not the old one, the one who used to press a thumb to
Nico's forehead and whisper gracia. That priest had disappeared last
year. No one had asked where.

This one kept his eyes low and his collar crisp. He never looked at the children.

One of the men had a tattoo of Santa Muerte inked across his chest—a robed skeleton weighing hearts. The other wore a silver chain with the Virgin dangling from it, her face darkened by sweat.

A girl lit a candle and crossed herself, as if none of it meant anything.

The fan above clicked in slow, uneven circles. Behind the altar, the crucifix sagged on its nails. The paint was flaking from Christ's face.

Nico watched everything. He remembered when the church smelled like incense and flowers. When the benches were full and people still sang.

Now, the silence was heavier than the music had ever been.

He stood and walked out.

Outside, the sun had dipped behind the hills, turning the sky the color of old bruises. The town glowed dimly—house lights flickering, dogs barking down alleyways, a motorbike sputtering in the distance.

He waited near the wall, beneath a mural of Saint Michael with his sword drawn.

After a while, he lowered himself to the curb cross-legged, watching the road.

Someone had spray-painted over it with a skull and the word respeta. Beneath it, in faded ink, someone had scrawled a name:

YAMA

Nico didn't know who had written it. But he'd seen it before—on a back wall of the mercado, on a folded slip of paper someone dropped and never returned for.

He'd asked his father once. The man didn't answer, just said, "You don't want to know about him."

They said he was a man, but no one said it with certainty. That he never raised his voice, but people lost their tongues just the same. That one boy came home without hands. That another didn't come home at all—just the boots.

Ten minutes later, his father emerged, wiping his hands with a cloth like he'd touched something unclean.

"I told you to stay home," he said.

"I wanted to see."

His father sighed. Looked out at the road.

"Don't say anything about what you saw."

Nico said nothing.

"You don't understand," the man went on. "These aren't choices. We do what we have to."

"I know what it is," Nico said. "It's not an offering."

His father turned. "Then what is it?"

"It's payment. For being left alone."

That landed like a slap. His father looked down, folded the cloth, and tucked it in his pocket. "You think you're better than me?"

"No," Nico said. "I think I remember who we were."

His father said nothing.

But under his breath, as they turned to walk home, Nico thought he heard him mutter:

"Pray he never says your name."

They didn't talk about it again.

The next morning came like all the others—thin light through the curtains, the smell of dust, the sound of a rooster no one owned.

Nico ate quietly while his father read the paper. He didn't look up.

There was an article about a man found near the edge of the canyon. No photo. No details. Just: "body unrecognizable."

Nico watched his father scan it, pause, then flip the page without a word.

The name Yama was never mentioned.

It never was.

He Should've Known

At school, Lalo was waiting near the steps with a bag of sunflower seeds and another story.

"You hear about the man in San Tobías?" he asked.

Nico shook his head.

"They say he was caught running his mouth. Bragging about something he shouldn't have. Three nights later, they found his tongue nailed to a fence post. Just the tongue. Nothing else."

Lalo grinned like it was a joke. But he kept glancing behind him.

"Was it Yama?" Nico asked.

His grin faded.

"You don't say his name out loud," he said. "It's bad luck. Like inviting him in."

Nico said nothing. Just looked out at the road.

On the way home, he passed the old bike shop. It had been shuttered since the accident—Pedro Cortés, the owner, found pinned between two trucks just outside town.

People said it was a fluke. But someone had left a note at the scene. No one ever said what it said. Only that it was folded clean, and had no name.

Nico's father once told him Pedro had taken something that wasn't his. A truck route. A favor. Something small. But the price had been large.

"He should've known better," was all he'd said.

That evening, Nico found his father in the kitchen, staring at the sink.

The faucet was dripping. A single stream.

Drop.

Drop.

Drop.

His hands were raw. Scrubbed past clean. The rag lay on the counter, damp and frayed.

"You need anything?" Nico asked.

The man shook his head but didn't look over.

Nico watched him for a moment longer, then stepped outside.

The mural of Saint Michael waited in the fading light.

Someone had tried to paint over it again. The skull still bled through the color.

YAMA.

Nico struck a match and watched the flame tremble in the wind.

He didn't know why he kept coming back here.

Only that the thought would not leave him.

Yama wants to see you.

He hadn't heard it spoken. Hadn't seen it written.

It had simply appeared, like something remembered from a dream.

Nico let the match burn down to his fingers before dropping it.

He stood there a long time after the flame went out.

At the Threshold

He woke before the sun.

The house was still dark, still silent. His father's door was closed, the hallway thick with the breath of sleeping things.

Nico dressed without thinking—shirt, jeans, shoes with dust in the soles—and stepped outside.

The air held a bite. The stars were fading into pale gray.

Far off, a rooster called, and somewhere beyond that, a single shot cracked through the morning.

He didn't flinch. Just walked.

He passed the old church. The candles inside flickered faintly through the glass, though no one seemed to light them anymore. The doors were chained now, except on Sundays.

An old man sweeping the front steps across the road paused when he saw Nico. His broom stopped mid-motion.

"You heading out that way?" the man asked.

Nico didn't answer.

The old man nodded like he already knew. He tapped two fingers to his chest, then his forehead—a half-blessing, or a ward against bad luck. Then he went back to sweeping.

At the edge of town, the pavement ended.

Nico sat on a crumbling wall where the road gave way to gravel and wind. From here, you could see the rise of the hills, the faint trail that led into the canyon.

He'd never been that far. No one he knew had.

The compound was somewhere out there—his compound. They called it The Mouth, though no one said why.

Maybe because people went in and were never heard from again.

Maybe because it spoke only once, and then swallowed you whole.

Yama wants to see you.

The words from the day before returned, uninvited.

He picked up a stone and turned it in his palm. It was dense, like it had a will of its own.

He didn't believe in monsters. Not really.

But there was something in that name—Yama—that made the air thinner, the birds quieter, the morning longer.

He looked toward the trail. The dirt path bent into the hills like a scar.

At the far end, something shimmered—not light, not shadow, but suggestion.

The kind of shimmer that comes before heat.

Or revelation.

He stood.

Then sat again.

There was no decision yet. No plan. Just a silence that kept growing.

By the time the sun crested the ridge, Nico was already walking back.

He passed the bakery just as the first tray of bread hit the counter. The woman behind the glass looked up, then looked away.

A boy sweeping the sidewalk paused as Nico passed. He muttered something to himself—maybe a name, maybe a prayer.

Nico didn't stop.

Someone waved from across the road. He didn't wave back.

The closer he got to home, the more everything felt blurred—not like a dream, but like something had slipped just slightly out of alignment.

The town was still there. The buildings still stood. But something had pulled back from it all. Like the world had exhaled and was waiting to see what he would do next.

Back at the house, the windows were still dark.

He didn't go inside right away.

He sat on the front step, turned the stone again in his pocket.

The weight felt right.

Not heavy.

Not light.

Just true.

The Compound

He left again just after dawn, without telling his father. There was no need.

The house had already gone silent in a new way—not the hush of sleep, but of surrender.

His father didn't rise. Didn't move. Just lay behind the door like a man who had already buried something.

Nico stepped out quietly, carrying nothing.

This time, the air was colder.

The trail curled into the hills, narrowing as it climbed.

The town faded behind him—not just in distance, but in weight. Its sounds, its walls, its small rules and bargains—they all slipped away.

He moved as if pulled.

The compound appeared slowly, like a thing half-revealed.

First the gate: tall, rusted, unmarked.

Then the walls—low, worn concrete, lined with glass shards cemented along the top.

Not to keep people out.

To keep something in.

A man waited at the gate. No words. No gun. Just a nod.

The gate opened. Nico entered.

Inside, it was quiet.

Too quiet.

No shouting. No trucks. No music.

Just the sound of wind through dry grass, and the buzz of distant electricity.

The buildings were low and square, made of pale brick and stained metal. Their edges were too clean—like the desert hadn't been allowed to weather them.

Someone brought him water in a plain cup.

Another handed him a folded towel.

A woman showed him to a room.

Small. Clean. Cot, table, chair.

A light that pulsed once every ten seconds.

No lock on the door.

No windows, either.

She left without speaking.

He sat on the cot.

The room felt like the inside of a held breath.

A few minutes passed.

Or maybe an hour.

There was no clock.

Then the door opened again.

A tray of food. Rice, beans, chicken. Still warm.

Next to it: a phone.

No cord. No label. Just a black screen.

He didn't touch it.

The light in the ceiling continued its pulse.

Ten seconds on. Ten off.

Nico lay back and watched it cycle until he lost track.

In the stillness, the stories returned. Not words. Images.

The man with no tongue.

The boots, still laced.

Pedro Cortés, his spine broken like a toy.

None of it had ever been confirmed.

But none had ever been denied.

They lived in the town like ghosts—untouched, unchallenged.

And now Nico was here,

where those stories pointed.

The First Temptation

The light was steady now.

No longer pulsing.

He didn't hear the door open.

She was just there.

No knock. No footsteps. No tray of food or folded towel. Just the soft shuffle of bare feet on tile, and the faint scent of rose and sandalwood.

She stood in the doorway for a moment, as if deciding whether to speak. Then stepped inside and closed the door behind her.

"I brought this," she said, holding up a bowl of water and a clean cloth.

Her voice was soft but grounded—neither shy nor forward.

Nico said nothing.

"I thought you might want to clean up."

He nodded once.

She set the bowl on the table, dipped the cloth, and wrung it out slowly, precisely, like it mattered. Then held out her hand.

"May I?"

He hesitated.

Then gave her his hand.

Her touch was careful.

Not clinical. Not flirtatious. Just deliberate.

She wiped the dust from his knuckles, under his nails, along the creases of his palm.

She took her time.

"You've come a long way," she said.

Still, he didn't speak.

She looked up. Her eyes were darker than he expected. Not sad, but seasoned. As if she'd watched too many people make the same mistake.

"You're not like the others," she said.

"The others?"

"They all come looking for something.

You're the first I've seen who already knows what he doesn't want."

He pulled his hand back gently.

She didn't resist.

Instead, she soaked the cloth again and reached up—slowly—touching it to his forehead, then his cheeks, his jawline.

Her fingers brushed the edge of his hair.

"You can rest here," she said. "You don't have to carry all that."

Her voice had changed.

Softer now.

Closer.

He felt the warmth of her breath near his cheek.

Then her hand found his knee.

Something in him stirred.

Not lust. Not yet. Just memory.

Of being held once, long ago, in the crook of someone's arm.

Of a lullaby sung without words.

Of touch not as desire, but as shelter.

She leaned in slightly—not forceful, but sure.

Her other hand moved to his shoulder, then paused—waiting, almost asking.

Her scent was stronger now.

Not perfume.

Something warm. Human. Living.

She brushed his hair back from his forehead, and for a moment, he imagined what would happen if he leaned in.

If he let the warmth take over.

If he stopped asking, and just accepted what was being offered.

He looked into her face.

It was kind.

Too kind.

As if it had been worn smooth from being offered too often.

"No," he said quietly. "I'm not here for comfort."

Her hand lingered on his shoulder a moment longer—then withdrew.

She didn't step back right away. Just stood in front of him, searching his face.

"You think that makes you strong?" she asked, her voice no longer soft.

He didn't answer.

She tilted her head, almost pitying. "It doesn't. It makes you alone."

Still, he said nothing.

The warmth between them evaporated, replaced by something colder.

She picked up the bowl slowly, as if each motion were a test of whether he'd call her back.

He didn't.

She walked to the door, then paused—half-turned.

"You'll wish you had taken something with you," she said.

But her voice had changed again.

No longer inviting.

No longer sad.

Now it sounded like a warning.

Then she left, and the door clicked softly behind her.

The silence that followed was thicker than before.

Nico sat still, as if the echo of her warmth still hovered in the air.

The chair. The table. The cot.

Everything was as it had been.

But something in the room had shifted.

As if it had opened and closed a door he hadn't seen.

He exhaled slowly.

Let his palms rest on his knees.

He didn't feel victorious.

Only more awake.

The Second Temptation

He wasn't sure if he had slept.

The cot was cool beneath him. The light in the ceiling had gone still again. No pulse. No hum. Just silence.

Then, in the corner of the room—something new. A faint glow.

It came from the table.

The phone.

He hadn't noticed it before. It hadn't been there. He was certain.

But now it lay face-up, dark screen flickering every ten seconds.

Like the ceiling light had.

Like everything in this place did—appearing not when needed, but when noticed.

Nico stared at it.

Didn't touch it.

Didn't move.

The first buzz came just after he sat down.

Short. Familiar.

He'd heard that sound a thousand times—once, it had meant friends, plans, normalcy. But here, it felt like something pulling a string inside his chest.

The screen lit up.

Lalo

No last name. Just the name.

He hesitated.

Then tapped the message.

"where are you? are you ok?"

His stomach tightened.

He hadn't thought of Lalo in days—not since the walk.

But the message didn't feel like a memory.

It felt recent.

Like it had just been written.

Another buzz.

A new name.

Ana

He blinked.

Ana had moved away years ago.

The last time he saw her was in front of the panadería, holding her mother's hand.

But her name was there, bright and casual.

"I heard you were back. We should talk."

He swiped again.

Photos now—grainy, but real.

One of him and Lalo sitting outside the shop.

One of his father on the porch.

One of himself, younger, before things turned quiet.

He tapped a voice message by accident.

The audio crackled, then spoke:

"Hey… it's me. Haven't seen you in forever. Just wondering if you're okay. It'd be good to hear your voice again."

It sounded real.

Too real.

He set the phone down, face down.

Stood.

Walked in a slow circle around the room.

Nothing had changed.

No new furniture. No hidden speaker.

Just that same pulsing silence—watchful, expectant.

He sat again.

The phone buzzed once more.

His father.

That one froze him.

He didn't tap it right away.

Didn't want to.

Did.

"I'm sorry for how I've been. Come home, mijo. Just come home."

His throat tightened.

He put the phone down gently.

But it buzzed again.

"Everything's forgiven. Just say yes. We'll make it right."

He looked around the room, half-expecting someone to be standing there, watching.

But it was empty.

The door closed.

The air still.

The phone was just a black rectangle again.

Harmless.

Ordinary.

He picked it up again.

Opened the camera.

No image.

Just black.

Then, faintly, his own face emerged. Dim. Uncentered. Not smiling.

He stared at it.

It stared back.

And then—

"You don't have to do this."

He didn't read the name attached to that one.

Because he already knew it was his own.

The temptation here wasn't comfort.

It was relief.

The idea that none of this had to matter.

That he could just leave.

That the world he left behind was still waiting, open-armed, unbroken.

It felt so easy.

Just say yes. Just say, I made a mistake.

The phone buzzed again.

He didn't look. Instead, he whispered—not to the phone, but to himself:

"No."

He held it in his palm for a while longer. Then set it down. Screen up.

It stopped buzzing.

The light dimmed.

And the room returned to its old, heavy stillness.

The Third Temptation

He hadn't eaten. The tray had come and gone. The woman didn't return. The phone stayed dark.

Then a knock. Not loud.

Just two short raps on the door.

A man stepped inside.

Mid-forties, maybe. Clean shirt, neatly tucked. Trim beard. Polished boots. Hands too clean for manual work.

He didn't carry a weapon, but he didn't need to.

His calm was its own kind of authority.

"Mind if I sit?" the man asked.

Nico said nothing.

The man sat anyway.

"Name's Emilio," he said, as if they were neighbors, or colleagues. "I work directly under Yama. When he wants something said clearly, he sends me."

Nico leaned back.

Emilio smiled faintly.

"You've done well," he said. "Not many get this far. Most fold after the first temptation. Even fewer make it past the second.

You… you're interesting."

Nico didn't respond.

"Look," Emilio said, resting his elbows on the table, "I'm not here to test you. I'm here to explain. You deserve that."

He reached into his coat and placed something on the table.

A set of keys. Three of them, on a leather strap.

One of them bore a truck logo.

Nico stared at them.

"This is yours," Emilio said. "If you want it."

He let the words settle.

"This isn't about bribery," he continued. "It's about recognition.

We see what you are. And we want you here."

"Why?"

"Because you're clear-eyed.

Because you don't scare easy.

Because you've suffered—quietly—and come out the other side still listening. That's rare."

Nico said nothing.

"This place runs on more than fear," Emilio said.

"It runs on structure. Precision. Roles.

We need people who can hold the line when everything else starts to blur."

He tapped the keys once.

"You could be that."

Nico looked down.

"What would I be?" he asked.

Emilio didn't miss a beat.

"Someone who sees things for what they are.

Someone who doesn't just survive but shapes.

We'd train you. Not just in how things move, but in why."

He paused.

"Yama believes in purpose. He doesn't waste people. Everyone here has a place."

"And if I say no?"

Emilio shrugged.

"You walk out. No one stops you. No threats. No punishment."

"But I'd know."

"Yes," Emilio said.

"You'd always wonder what you turned down."

He reached into his jacket again.

This time, a folder.

Inside: photographs.

Nico's school.

His street.

His father.

Lalo.

A local cop.

A shipment.

A ledger.

All taken from angles that suggested they had always been watching.

"This world isn't what you think," Emilio said.

"Everyone plays a part. Some know it. Some don't.

But everyone chooses."

He tapped the keys again.

"This is a different kind of power.

Not brute. Not loud.

But real.

The kind that doesn't need to raise its voice."

Nico's eyes returned to the keys.

They were small. Unremarkable.

They wouldn't change him, not on the outside.

But something in them called to that part of him that wanted to understand.

To know how the world actually worked.

To see the gears beneath the illusion.

He imagined holding them.

Slipping them into his pocket.

Letting the structure wrap around him like armor.

No more questions.

No more wandering.

Just function.

He reached out.

Let his fingers brush the edge of the leather strap.

Then withdrew.

"I'm not here for power," he said.

Emilio's eyes didn't narrow. Didn't even blink.

But something behind them sharpened.

"Most people say that," he said.

"Right before they take it."

He stood, slower this time. Not with calm, but with restraint.

Folded the folder back into his coat—deliberately.

Almost too deliberately.

Like someone reining something in.

Then he gestured toward the keys—still on the table.

"One more night," he said.

But now the words felt thinner, stretched.

"After that, you'll know."

He turned toward the door, paused, then looked back—not with warning,

but with the smallest flicker of frustration.

"You think this is about virtue?" he said.

"You'll learn. We all do."

Then he left, the door clicking shut with just a bit more force than before.

Nico sat in the quiet.

The keys remained.

Simple. Elegant. Entirely possible.

He looked at them for a long time.

Then turned them over, once.

And left them there.

He didn't sleep.

The room no longer felt neutral—it felt watched.

Not with cameras or eyes,

but with something older.

Like the space itself had learned to listen.

The door opened just after midnight.

Not with ceremony.

Just a quiet click,

and then Emilio entered again—same clean shirt, same calm presence.

But this time, he carried nothing in his hands.

"You said no to comfort," he said.

"No to connection.

And now, no to clarity."

He sat across from Nico again.

No smile this time. Just stillness.

"You're running out of things to refuse."

Nico didn't answer.

Emilio leaned forward, elbows on the table.

"You think this is about strength. About saying no.

But it's not.

It's about what you're saying yes to."

He paused.

"Tomorrow, Yama will see you.

That's not a meeting.

That's a crossing.

You'll either step forward or vanish.

There's no middle."

He rose.

Stared down at the keys one last time, then turned to go.

At the door, he said, "Once you see clearly, you can't ever go back to being blind."

Then he left.

Nico sat alone.

He didn't touch the keys.

But they remained in the corner of his eye.

Shining dully.

Like something simple and sacred,

waiting to be chosen.

The Visit

He felt it before he heard anything.

The room shifted.

Not in light or temperature, but in density—

as if the air itself had been pulled tight.

Like the pause before a storm,

when everything leans forward but nothing moves.

The Nico realized

He was no longer alone.

Yama.

No guards.

No shadow behind him.

Just a man in a crisp, dark shirt and slacks, sleeves rolled once at the cuffs.

His hair was long, silvering.

His face unreadable—not cold, not warm. Just… settled.

Like it had been still for a very long time.

He didn't look around. He looked straight at Nico.

"You've done well," he said.

As if he had been watching the entire time.

His voice was low, steady.

It didn't ask for attention. It didn't need to.

He sat across from Nico, folding his hands neatly on the table.

No introductions. No questions.

"You haven't eaten."

Nico shook his head.

Yama tilted his own slightly.

"Good. Hunger sharpens the senses."

They sat in silence for a while.

Yama didn't fill it.

He simply watched Nico.

Not like a predator. More like a surgeon studying a scan.

Looking for the shape inside the shape.

Then he asked:

"Do you know what brought you here?"

Nico didn't answer.

Yama nodded, as if that were the answer.

"They all say different things.

Loyalty. Curiosity. Grief."

He paused.

"Some come chasing revenge.

Some think this place holds secrets they can use."

He leaned back slightly.

"But you.

You're different.

You didn't come for answers.

You came for truth."

Nico looked at him then.

Really looked.

Yama was neither young nor old.

His face was without fatigue, but heavy with something else—accumulation, perhaps.

Like he carried the stories of everyone who'd ever sat across from him.

"What is this place?" Nico asked.

"A mouth," Yama said.

"It speaks once, then swallows."

"Swallows what?"

"Whatever's left after truth has spoken."

Nico felt his chest tighten.

He didn't know if it was fear.

Or something older.

Yama glanced at the door. Then back.

"They've tempted you," he said.

"The body. The heart. The mind.

You said no."

"It wasn't hard," Nico said.

"No?" Yama raised an eyebrow.

"Then you weren't listening."

He stood.

Walked once around the table, slow, unhurried.

He stopped beside Nico, then leaned in—not threateningly,
just close enough for his words to feel private.
"They offered you things you already wanted.
That's the trick."
He stepped back.
"But it's the self that must be tempted last."
Nico blinked.
"What do you mean?"
"I mean you think you're here to ask questions.
But really, you're here to be asked."
Yama moved to the far corner of the room and opened a cabinet
Nico hadn't noticed before.
From it, he took something wrapped in cloth.
He placed it on the table.
Unwrapped it.
A stone.
Smooth. Palm-sized.
It gleamed.
Like it had a memory of being seen.
Yama nodded toward it.
"Pick it up."
Nico reached for it.
Hesitated.
Then lifted it.
It was heavy.
Much heavier than it should have been for its size.
He looked up.
Yama watched him with no expression.
"That stone," he said,
"was taken from a place where no names survive.

It has passed through many hands.
Some kings.
Some killers.
Some who thought they were both."
Nico held it in his palm.
It seemed to pull inward,
as if swallowing light.
"What is it?" he asked.
"A reminder," Yama said.
"That not everything that endures is alive.
And not everything alive is real."
Nico set it down slowly.
Yama sat again.
"You've already begun," he said.
"The moment you crossed the hill,
you left your name behind."
"I still know who I am."
Yama smiled.
It wasn't cruel.
It was almost kind.
"No.
You only know who you were."
They sat for a long while in silence.
Then Yama rose again.
"One more night," he said.
"Then we'll talk about what cannot be spoken."
He walked to the door, placed a hand on the knob, and paused.
"Don't sleep too deeply."
And then he was gone.

An Unraveling

He didn't remember falling asleep.

He only remembered waking.

The stone was still on the table.

The keys, untouched.

The room exactly as it had been.

Except he wasn't alone.

Yama sat in the corner, legs crossed, back straight as a blade.

His hands rested lightly on his knees, and he was watching
Nico—not intensely, but patiently,

like someone observing a fire take hold.

"You dream," Yama said,

"but you don't confuse it for something else.

That's rare."

Nico rubbed his eyes.

"Were you here all night?"

"I'm always here. Just not always seen."

Yama stood and walked toward the table.

He didn't sit. Just looked down at the stone.

"You're still holding on," he said.

"To what?" asked Nico.

Yama looked up.

"To yourself."

He said it so plainly, it didn't even feel like an accusation.

"Who do you think you are?" he asked.

Nico said nothing.

Yama tilted his head.

"Go on. Tell me the story you call yourself."

Nico's jaw tightened.

"I'm no one special."

"Good start," Yama said.

"Now strip away your name.

Your birthplace.

Your memories.

Take off each layer like clothing you forgot you were wearing.

What's left?"

Nico frowned.

"Nothing?" he offered.

Yama's eyes lit, faintly.

"Almost."

He picked up the stone and rolled it between his palms.

"You think you are your memories," Yama said.

Nico frowned.

"Which one?" Yama asked.

He set the stone back down.

"Listen," he said.

Nico shifted in his seat.

"Then what dies?" asked Nico.

Yama smiled.

"What dies," Yama said, "is the story."

"And what doesn't?"

Yama stepped closer.

"The seer."

They stood in silence.

Yama's voice lowered.

"You've spent your whole life polishing the mirror.

But you've never asked what's looking through it."

Nico looked away.

Everything in him wanted to argue.

He thought of his father.

His mother.

The girl in the church.

He thought of the street he grew up on.

The sound of dogs at night.

The warmth of his grandmother's bread.

He reached for it.

But it slipped.

Like smoke.

Like a dream.

"You've done well to resist," Yama said.

"Most want comfort. Some want control.

But very few want truth."

"Why?"

Yama's eyes darkened, just a shade.

"Because truth costs everything that isn't real."

He returned to the corner.

Sat cross-legged again.

"You're not being tested anymore," he said.

"This isn't a trial."

"Then what is it?"

Yama looked at him.

"You already know," Yama said quietly

Nico didn't ask what it meant.

He knew, in a way that bypassed language,

that he had always known,

That every unease,

every longing,

every question—

had been the pull of that remembering.

He exhaled.

Long and slow.

And the room, for the first time, felt spacious.

"You still have one more night," Yama said.

"One more for what?"

"To die properly."

He stood and walked to the door.

Paused.

Then turned back.

"When you wake," he said,

"we'll see what remains."

He opened the door.

And this time, when he left,

the room didn't feel smaller.

It felt hollowed.

Like something had been carved out.

Something that had never belonged there.

The Last Night

The room was empty.

No food.

No visitors.

No keys.

No stone.

Even the chair Yama had used was gone.

As if the room had never belonged to him at all.

Nico stood in the center, listening.

But there was nothing left to hear—not even the hum behind silence.

Just stillness, so complete it began to feel like weight.

He stepped outside.

The hallway seemed longer than before.

Shadows reached where they shouldn't.

The doors looked like doors, but they no longer felt like entrances.

Just shapes pretending to have depth.

He walked.

The compound had changed. Not in any way he could explain.

But everything seemed one step removed from itself.

The walls curved differently.

The sky felt too close.

The wind moved without touching anything.

He thought of the woman's last words:

You'll wish you had taken something with you.

Maybe she was right.

Maybe he already had.

He reached the courtyard.

It was brighter than it should've been, lit by a moon that didn't cast shadows.

The gravel underfoot made no sound.

He sat on a low wall, knees drawn up, arms wrapped around them.

Not to keep warm.

To keep together.

Because something in him had begun to loosen.

Not like a thread unraveling—

but like a knot forgetting why it was tight.

He tried to remember his name.

It came slowly.

Then it left again.

There were no stars overhead.

Just a sky that felt distant.

He closed his eyes.

For a moment, there was only breath.

Then a voice.

Not Yama's.

Not anyone's.

Just a voice, like the one that had been asking all along.

If you are not your name…

If you are not your past…

…then what remains?

He didn't answer.

There was no one left to answer.

The stone was in his hand.

He didn't remember picking it up.

But there it was—

heavy, smooth, warm.

He stared at it.

And for the first time,

it didn't feel like an object.

It felt like a question.

The sky dimmed slightly.

He stood.

Walked past the gate.

Past the outer wall.

Out into the sand.

He didn't look back.

Not once.

The desert was waiting.

Not vast.
Not cruel.
Just… there.
Like a witness
with nothing left to record.
Each step felt quieter than the last,
not because the world hushed,
but because he did.
The burden of shape,
of story,
of effort—
draining gently,
like ink dissolving in water.
He no longer wondered if he'd find Yama again.
He no longer wondered what came next.
He simply walked.
At some point, he stopped.
The stone was gone.
Or maybe his hand was.
He looked down at his hands.
They were empty.
He sat down, cross-legged,
facing nothing in particular.
And closed his eyes.
He didn't fall asleep.
But something ended.
And something else—
something vast and silent—
opened in its place.
He closed his eyes.

He didn't fall asleep.
But something ended.
And something vast and silent opened in its place.

WHAT CANNOT BURN

The Letter

Bavarian Alps, Autumn 1933

He had not spoken aloud in three days, but now, the envelope in his hand demanded a sound. Something—anything. He opened his mouth. Nothing came.

The wax seal was cracked, the paper slightly damp from the climb the boy had made to bring it. A letter. From Leipzig.

He set it beside the cold kettle and stared at it as if it might disappear if he waited long enough.

Outside, the valley held its breath. The larch trees below had begun to yellow, their color faint against the granite sky. Smoke lifted from a dozen homes and curled across the late-afternoon light. Nothing unusual. And yet everything felt off, like a prayer said backward.

He opened the letter.

Dieter—

Forgive me for using that name. I know you've left it behind. But I don't know what else to call you when I write from this world. They are burning books now. University lectures end in silence— not because they're finished, but because no one dares speak. The streets are full of uniforms. Not just soldiers. Everyone. They watch what you buy. What you read. Who you sit with. I write because I still remember who you were, and because I fear they may not allow such men to exist much longer.

Leave, Devananda. Or hide. Just don't think yourself invisible. The light you carry is not as quiet as you think.

He folded the letter with deliberate care, as if the act of returning it to stillness might still the mind as well. Then he sat with it.

"They are burning books now."

He remembered a saying passed between mendicants in Rishikesh:

Tamas burns first what it does not understand. Then what it cannot control.

He did not fear for himself—not in the usual way. His body was no longer precious. But the air felt charged with something he hadn't tasted in years. Restlessness. The mind trying to move ahead of the moment.

Should I leave now?

Would that be wisdom or fear?

And if I stay… what then?

The silence of the hut, which had long comforted him, felt dense now. Like something waiting.

He rose, folded the letter again, and slipped it inside a small pouch tucked into the wall beam. Then he boiled water, though he no longer wanted tea. He dressed in his plain gray robe, wrapped a wool shawl across his shoulders, and stepped outside.

The wind was thin and cold. A crow flapped past him without cawing.

The Valley Below

The trail into the village was steep but familiar. The stones shifted beneath his sandals, reminding him of the body's impermanence— how easily it might fall, how little it mattered.

He entered the village just as the sun began to withdraw. The baker's sign creaked faintly in the breeze. A woman, headscarf tight, moved briskly past him without nodding. That was new. Last year, she'd invited him for tea.

A boy was chalking something on the wall near the church. Devananda slowed to read it as he passed.

"Germany Awakened."

A swastika, uneven but bold, looped beneath it.

The boy looked at him, then at the ground.

At the grocer's, a new man stood behind the counter—young, neat, blond. He did not greet Devananda, only waited. Devananda selected a few potatoes and a pouch of barley.

The clerk glanced at him, then down at the coins.

"You're not from here," he said flatly.

"I've lived here for many years," Devananda replied.

"But not from here."

Devananda smiled gently. "Does it matter?"

The man didn't answer. He wrapped the barley and placed it on the counter with more force than needed. Devananda bowed slightly, accepted the bundle, and left.

Outside, he noticed two men standing near the well. They wore no uniforms, but one of them carried a small notebook and occasionally scribbled in it. The other just watched.

As Devananda passed, one of them muttered, "That's him."

He kept walking. He didn't turn.

The walk back was quieter than the descent. The sun had slipped fully behind the ridge, leaving the valley in bluish shadow. He heard only his breath and the clink of stones underfoot.

He arrived at his hut just before full dark. The trees whispered. Something unseen moved in the underbrush. Or perhaps it was nothing.

Inside, he lit a lamp and sat by the window. He closed his eyes to meditate, but the stillness was no longer pure. A tension throbbed beneath it—a question that refused to quiet:

Am I here to witness, or to act?

If it is all the play of the *gunas*, then who am I to stop it?

But if compassion arises, can I ignore it and still claim to know what I am?

The mind stirred. The breath wavered. And for the first time in many years, Devananda felt himself caught—not between right and wrong, but between clarity and confusion.

He opened his eyes and whispered, "May the truth become clear before the hour is too late."

Then he blew out the lamp and sat again, not seeking silence, but waiting for the storm to enter it.

Three Strands of the Same Rope

Rishikesh, Some Years Earlier

The heat was sharp even in the morning. The ashram courtyard lay in dappled light, shaded by a neem tree that crackled with bird-song and the faint scent of smoke. Dieter—still new to silence, still uncertain of his place—sat cross-legged among the others, waiting for the swami to speak.

He had come to India half out of disillusionment and half out of defiance. His professors had warned him he was wasting his mind. "Mysticism is the opiate of thinkers," one had sneered. But the more he read of Shankara and the Upanishads, the more he felt the hard angles of Western thought dissolve. Here, nothing was separate. Not even pain.

The swami arrived barefoot, his ochre robe brushing the ground like wind on cloth. He sat on a low platform, his eyes quiet but alert, like someone listening to music only he could hear.

He began without preamble.

"There is no such thing as a good world or a bad world," he said.

"There are only the *gunas*—*sattva, rajas, tamas*. Three strands of one rope. The rope of prakriti, of nature itself. Everything you see, feel, think, even dream—made of these three."

Dieter shifted slightly on the mat. The other students sat like stone.

The swami looked directly at him.

"You are from Germany, yes? What is your name?"

"Dieter," he said, then corrected himself. "Devananda."

The swami nodded. "Ah. Joy of the divine. It fits. But for now, you are still Dieter."

A few students chuckled. Devananda smiled, faintly.

"Dieter," the swami said, "do you sometimes feel clear, like everything is light?"

"Yes," he replied.

"And then sometimes full of energy, craving, passion, motion?"

"Yes."

"And other times dull, confused, like you're sinking into mud?"

He hesitated, then nodded.

"These are not your moods," the swami said. "They are the weather of the mind. They pass through you, but they are not you. Just the *gunas*—*sattva, rajas, tamas*. Clarity. Activity. Inertia."

He picked up a long thread from the floor—three strands twisted together.

"They are always woven. Never one alone. The question is not which one is there. The question is, do you identify with it?"

Dieter leaned forward. "If they are impersonal, then what of cruelty? Or violence?"

"Ah," the swami said. "Now you are asking with the fire of dharma."

He stood and walked slowly to the edge of the platform.

"Even cruelty is born of the *gunas*. When *tamas* dominates—when there is no light to see the effect of one's action, and *rajas* fuels the will to act anyway—then destruction comes. Not because a man is evil, but because he does not know what else he is. He thinks he is his thoughts, his fear, his pride. And so he obeys them."

"But if he sees—truly sees—that it is not personal, then freedom begins."

Dieter felt something crack in him, like a window opening inside the chest.

"So there is no one to hate?" he asked.

The swami smiled gently. "Only ignorance to understand."

That night, Devananda had written in his journal:

There are no monsters. Only clouds blocking the sun. The question is not how to kill the clouds, but how to remember the sky.

He opened his eyes. The memory faded, replaced by the soft hiss of pine needles brushing the side of the hut. Outside, the valley was still and blue with early morning.

He sat alone with the kettle, thinking of the swami, of those words spoken in heat and light. He had believed, then, that understanding was enough. That knowing the *gunas* would keep him clear forever.

But now…Now the rope pulled at him in ways he could not name. Now he felt the strands twist around the world.

A Knock in the Mist

The mist came early that morning, thick and low like breath

held against the skin of the valley. The world was gray and wet and silent.

Devananda sat near the hearth, the kettle warming, his thoughts nowhere in particular. The letter had not moved from its pouch, but its weight had not left the room.

He was just beginning to rise when the knock came.

Not loud. Three soft taps. Hesitant, like someone unsure if a knock still meant welcome.

He paused. Few ever came to the hut unannounced. Fewer still climbed the trail in mist.

When he opened the door, a girl stood there—perhaps ten years old, wrapped in a threadbare coat two sizes too large. Her cheeks were red from cold. Her dark hair stuck to her face like rain-soaked threads.

She said nothing.

Devananda waited.

After a moment, she reached into her coat and pulled out a cloth bundle. She held it out with both hands.

He took it.

A loaf of bread, still warm. No name. No note.

Just the silence between them—and something unspoken behind her eyes.

He looked at her.

"From the baker's wife?" he asked gently.

The girl nodded.

"She said to thank you for the herbs. She said you saved her son's lungs."

He hadn't known the boy was her son. He had only given herbs, instructions, and silence.

"Would you like tea?" he asked.

The girl hesitated, then nodded.

Inside, she sat cross-legged on the mat near the fire, hands cupped around the warm clay cup. She didn't drink right away.

"My uncle says you're a holy man," she said after a while.

"I wear these robes," Devananda replied.

"He also says you're dangerous."

Devananda smiled softly. "He may be right."

The girl frowned. "But you gave us herbs. And you don't have guns. How can that be dangerous?"

He stirred the fire with a piece of pine branch, watching the sparks spiral upward.

"There are many kinds of danger," he said. "Some are loud and quick. Some are quiet and slow. Some live in the body. Some live in the mind."

"Like books?" she asked. "They burned books at the school."

He looked at her then—not with surprise, but with a kind of sadness he kept beneath the skin.

"Yes," he said. "Like books."

"Why?"

He took a breath and let it out slowly.

"Because people are afraid of things that don't move the way they want."

She looked down. "Will they burn the people too?"

He didn't answer right away.

"No," he said finally. "Not yet."

When she left, she bowed in the awkward way of a child mimicking what she's seen adults do. He bowed in return, not as a ritual, but as gratitude—for the bread, and for the question that still burned.

After she disappeared into the mist, Devananda stood outside for a long time, staring into the trees.

A sick child. A loaf of bread, he thought. This is how it begins.

And then, the voice in him whispered again:

If the fire spreads, can you still sit beside it and not reach for a pail?

He returned to the hut and sat. But the silence had changed again.

This time, it wasn't the letter.

This time, it was the weight of eyes beginning to look to him—not for doctrine, not for miracles, but for the simple question of what one does when the world begins to break.

The Man from Leipzig

It was near dusk when he heard footsteps—confident ones. Not the shuffle of a villager or the tentative knock of a child.

He opened the door before the man could knock.

"Dieter!" the man beamed, arms wide. "God, look at you. It's been… what, ten years?"

Devananda blinked. For a moment, he didn't know whether to speak.

"Mathias," he said finally. "From the university."

"The very same," Mathias said, brushing past him with the ease of someone who had once shared wine and long nights arguing over Kant. "You haven't aged a day."

"I've aged," Devananda said, closing the door. "Just differently."

The man looked around the hut with mild amusement. "So this is the hermitage. I always thought you'd end up in some cave in India."

"I was in caves. This is warmer."

Mathias laughed and sat uninvited on the bench by the hearth.

He looked healthy, dressed in a fine wool coat, boots that had barely touched mud. His eyes still carried the same spark—quick, restless—but there was something else now. A tightness. A glint.

"I was in the area for work," Mathias said. "Thought I'd try my luck. I heard rumors of a 'German monk' living in the hills. Figured it had to be you."

Devananda poured water into the kettle. "What work brings you to a place like this?"

"Consulting. Policy work. I'm advising a regional office now. Educational reform."

The way he said "reform" made Devananda pause.

Mathias leaned forward. "I read your essay once. The one about detachment and the illusion of self. You always had the soul of a mystic—even when you were still quoting Schopenhauer."

Devananda smiled faintly. "Some truths don't need replacing. Only seeing."

Mathias nodded thoughtfully, then added, "But of course, seeing is a privilege. Not everyone can afford to rise above the world. Some of us have to build it."

The kettle hissed softly.

Devananda handed him a cup.

There was silence.

Then: "You're aware, I imagine, of how things are shifting. It's not like it was."

"I've noticed," Devananda said.

"There's fear, yes," Mathias continued, "but there's also… opportunity. We're cleaning house. Making room for strength. Order. Unity."

The words landed like river stones—smooth on the outside, but meant to sink.

"And this?" Mathias gestured at the hut. "This retreat—how long do you think it will remain safe? Things are tightening. We're watching for subversive ideas, foreign influences. You wouldn't want to be mistaken for… something else."

Devananda said nothing.

Mathias sipped the tea. "You could come back, you know. Speak. Teach. There are people who'd listen now—hungry for meaning. You could frame it well. In alignment with the new vision. You wouldn't have to hide."

Devananda looked at him, really looked. Not at the man, but at a kind of impersonal force wearing the man like clothing. The *gunas* at work.

Not evil. Just twisted. Just dimmed.

"Mathias," he said softly, "do you remember what we said that night in Dresden, when the rector denied funding to the Jewish scholars?"

Mathias blinked. "I remember shouting."

"You said, 'Truth has no uniform.'"

Mathias looked away. "Yes, well. The world has uniforms now. One must adapt."

He finished his tea, stood, and brushed off invisible dust.

"I should go. The roads aren't safe after dark. But you—just think about what I said. You still have time to step forward. Before someone decides you've stepped aside."

He placed the cup down with a little too much care.

"It was good to see you, Dieter."

"I go by Devananda now."

Mathias paused, smiled faintly.

"Of course you do."

The Stranger Beneath the Ash Tree

Days passed.

The forest returned to silence.

Devananda spent his mornings splitting wood, his afternoons walking the ridge. He meditated as the sun dipped low, and slept with the fire near his feet.

The letter sat untouched. So did the memory of the girl, and the man from Leipzig.

But silence, as he had learned, is never empty.

He felt it again—before sound came. A presence. Still and waiting.

This time, he opened the door without hesitation.

A boy—no, a man, though not much more—stood hunched beneath a cloak heavy with dew. His hair was matted, a thin line of blood marked one brow. Behind him, the ash trees whispered, almost protectively.

"I'm sorry," the man said. "I didn't know where else to go."

He spoke with a Saxon accent, but the voice was cracked by hunger and exhaustion.

Devananda said nothing. He stepped aside.

The man entered, eyes darting, as if still expecting pursuit. He hovered just inside the door, uncertain whether this sanctuary was real.

"There's water by the window," Devananda said, returning to the hearth. "And a blanket in the trunk."

The man hesitated, then drank. When he sat, he did so with a groan—his ribs must have been bruised. The blanket clung to his shoulders like a confession.

For a while, neither spoke.

Then, quietly, the man said, "They beat me for walking on the wrong road. There's a curfew now. I didn't know."

Devananda looked at him.

"Or maybe they knew who I was," the man continued, staring at his hands. "My father wrote something once. About the Reichstag fire. They never forgot."

Silence returned.

Outside, a crow called.

"What do you need?" Devananda asked.

The man swallowed. "Just sleep. One night. I'll be gone before light."

Devananda nodded. He stood and poured a little barley into a pot.

The boy watched him. "They say you're a monk."

"I am."

"Not Christian?"

"No."

"What kind, then?"

Devananda stirred the water. "The kind that watches fire without needing to put it out."

The boy looked at him, confused. But he said nothing more.

They ate in silence.

When the boy finally curled on the floor, blanket drawn over his head like a burial cloth, Devananda sat again at the hearth.

He did not sleep.

He thought of the ash trees outside—how some lose their leaves late, some early. How some split from lightning but live on.

He thought of the letter. The girl with the bread. The acquaintance from Leipzig.

And now this.

Not a blaze. Just a spark.

But even wildfires begin this way.

He closed his eyes, not to escape—but to see more clearly.

The boy's breathing deepened. In the quiet, Devananda whispered—not to the boy, but to the dark:

"Let me not confuse stillness with indifference."

The Encounter with a Villager

The boy was gone by dawn, just as he'd promised. Left behind was the folded blanket, still warm. And a single word carved into the frost on the windowpane:

Danke

Devananda stood before it, unmoving.

Later that morning, he walked to the stream. The air smelled of ash and iron.

Halfway down the slope, a familiar voice startled him.

"You still walk like a monk," said Frau Elze.

She was older than most, with strong shoulders and the steady gaze of someone who'd outlived every one of her brothers. She had been kind to him when he first arrived, offering a spade for the garden and jars of pickled cabbage in winter. But lately, she had kept her distance.

Today, she looked directly at him.

"Someone saw your lamp last night," she said. "Said there was movement."

He waited.

She sighed. "You don't have to explain. Just know that the road between here and the village is thinner than it used to be. Words travel."

He nodded.

"They're looking for anyone who shelters cowards. Or thinkers." She spat the word like it tasted of rot.

"Is that what he was?" Devananda asked gently.

"I don't care what he was," she said. "But they do."

She shifted her basket to the other hip. "There was a time people kept their heads down. Now they turn each other in for thinking too loudly."

Devananda watched a hawk circling high above the field.

"They haven't forgotten who you are," she added. "A foreign robe, a foreign God."

"I never brought either," he said. "Only silence."

"Doesn't matter. They'll hear what they want to hear."

She softened. "You've been good to us. But kindness won't shield you anymore. I'm telling you this because I don't want to see you vanish."

She touched his arm—just once—and turned back toward the village.

Devananda stood there a long while, until the wind shifted and the hawk drifted west.

The Dream of Fire and Water

That night, sleep did not come easily.

Devananda lay on his side, listening to the wind comb through the trees like fingers through hair. The hut creaked. Somewhere beyond, a fox screamed like a wounded child. And beneath it all: stillness. Too still.

Eventually, exhaustion overtook thought.

He dreamed of a dry riverbed. He stood barefoot where water

should have been. The sky was yellow. The trees were skeletal. A flame burned steadily in his chest—not painful, but bright, like a coal buried deep in ash.

He walked.

Along the banks, he saw villagers—men, women, children—digging at the soil with their hands, mouths parched. They didn't see him. Their eyes were clouded, as if turned inward. One struck the ground until his knuckles bled, whispering something in a language Devananda could almost understand.

He knelt beside a girl, no older than ten, who had collapsed in the dust. Her skin was cracked like clay. She looked at him and mouthed something.

He leaned closer.

"Is this the world you renounced?" she asked.

He stepped back.

Suddenly, a wall of flame rose between them—silent, hot, impersonal. The child vanished behind it. Then the villagers, one by one, turned toward the fire—not away from it, but into it—walking forward as if drawn by something deeper than fear.

Devananda called out, but his voice made no sound.

Then, another voice came—low, unmistakable, from behind his own eyes:

"You say the fire is not yours. But you were born of it, too.

You do not feed it. You do not flee it.

You sit beside it.

And that, too, is karma."

He turned and saw no one.

Only the dry riverbed.

And above it, a sky that began to rain—not water, but ash.

He awoke before dawn, sweat clinging to him like a second robe.

Outside, the forest was still.

But the silence no longer felt like sanctuary.

It felt like the moment before a match is struck.

Smoke in the Trees

The forest was damp that morning, yet something sharp hung in the air.

Devananda stepped outside, kettle in hand, and paused mid-step.

There was smoke—not from his chimney, but thin threads of it rising through the trees beyond the ridge. Not fire. Not yet. But close enough to smell.

He walked the trail slowly, listening.

When he crested the ridge, he saw them: three men in uniform, walking single file along the road that skirted the woods. One carried a lantern, another a rifle, and the third—short, stern-faced—tacked up a paper on a tree with quick, precise movements.

They didn't look in his direction. But they didn't need to.

By the time Devananda reached the tree, they were gone.

The paper flapped slightly in the breeze. Its words were brief, large, and unmistakable:

"Sheltering enemies of the state will be treated as treason."

Below, a list of names. He did not recognize them.

But he didn't need to.

The message was clear. And it had reached him.

He stood there for a long time. Watching the ink dry.

That evening, he swept the hut, as he always did. He made rice, as he always did. But something had changed. He felt it in his spine—an alertness, a silence no longer sacred but watchful.

After his meal, he lit the oil lamp and sat, facing the window.

He let his hand rest on his knee. The posture was familiar. But the stillness was not.

In his mind, he returned—not to the dream—but to something earlier. A voice in a dusty courtyard in Varanasi. His teacher's voice, when he was still young and full of zeal:

"The *gunas* must play, Devananda. Even *tamas*. Even *rajas*.

This world does not run on light alone."

He hadn't understood then. He had only nodded.

But tonight, sitting in a country far from that courtyard, the words came alive.

"The world exists only because the *gunas* are allowed to dance.

Deny one, and the play ends.

Even monsters have mothers."

The Man with the Scar

It was just after sundown when the knock came.

Not the tentative tap of a child or the panicked pounding of someone pursued. A firm, deliberate knock.

Three times. Then silence.

Devananda stood.

He did not reach for the lamp. He did not call out. He opened the door.

The man who stood there was tall, broad-shouldered, with a long gray coat and a flat cap pulled low. His face was lean, weathered, and marked by a thin scar that ran from his temple to the edge of his mouth. Not fresh. Not old. A scar that spoke of survival, not heroism.

They looked at each other for a long time.

"You don't know me," the man said.

Devananda nodded. "But you know me."

The man glanced over his shoulder, then back. "I was told you don't ask questions."

"I try not to," Devananda said. "But the mind is restless."

The man stepped inside without being asked.

He removed his coat and sat down without a word. There was something practiced in the way he moved—like someone used to living on the edge of exposure.

They sat in silence for a few minutes.

Then the man spoke.

"There's a train tomorrow. Midnight. They say it's the last. After that, the border's sealed. I don't want to be on it."

Devananda didn't respond.

"I've done things," the man continued. "Things I believed in. Things I don't. Doesn't matter now. They've turned on me. Called me a traitor."

He looked up, his eyes dark but clear.

"I'm not asking for shelter. I'm asking what a man should do when he finally sees the machine he built is crushing the wrong people."

Devananda met his gaze.

"The machine always crushes the wrong people," he said softly. "Sometimes even the ones who built it."

The man gave a bitter laugh. "I thought you were a monk. That sounds like politics."

"It's not," Devananda replied. "It's karma."

A long silence.

Then the man leaned forward.

"Tell me this," he said. "If you were me… would you run? Or stay and try to make it right?"

Devananda didn't answer. He studied the man's face, the scar, the steady hands, the weight behind his words.

At last, he said, "I'm not you."

"But you've seen what's coming."

"Yes."

"Then help me see it too."

Devananda looked down at his hands.

They were old hands. Browned by sun, wrinkled by time, steady from years of stillness. Once, he had thought they were no longer of use to the world. But now they trembled—just slightly—with the weight of someone else's crossroads.

He lifted his eyes.

"You want an answer," he said. "But you already know what you want to do. You came here to ask if it's allowed."

The man frowned.

"I came because I don't trust myself."

Devananda nodded slowly.

"That's a start."

He stood and poured two cups of water. The clay cups clinked softly. The fire crackled in its stone ring.

"When I first came to the path," he said, "my teacher told me something I didn't understand. He said, 'We renounce action not to avoid it, but to see it clearly.'"

"And can you see clearly now?"

Devananda met his eyes.

"Clear enough to know that clarity doesn't always bring comfort."

He sat across from the man.

"You are not here to be forgiven. You're here to decide what kind of man you want to be, now that your story has cracked open."

The man shifted. "But what if I choose wrong?"

"Then you live that consequence. And then, if you're still alive, you choose again."

He paused.

"This is the world of the *gunas*. There is no perfect choice. Only a choice made in light or in shadow."

The man stared into his cup.

"So what would you do?"

Devananda let the silence breathe before answering.

"If I thought I could stop one life from being crushed, I would act. Not to be a savior. Not to make things right. But because compassion does not wait for certainty."

He added, "But if I acted only to escape guilt, I would be doing it for myself. And that, too, is bondage."

The man closed his eyes.

When he opened them again, they were different—less frantic, more resolved.

"Thank you," he said, standing. "I don't know what I'll do yet. But I think I know how to listen now."

He paused at the door.

"You're not what I expected."

Devananda smiled faintly. "Neither are you."

The man vanished into the trees, his coat catching the last light of dusk.

Devananda remained at the threshold for a long time.

In the distance, the wind picked up. Ash trees hissed like old men arguing. The silence did not return. Not fully.

"We are not asked to fix the world," he whispered. "Only to do what is right when the moment arrives."

He turned back inside. The lamp flickered. The fire had burned low.

When the Fire Spreads

The sky cracked open at dawn.

Not with thunder, but with silence too loud to ignore. The birds did not sing. The village bell did not ring. And the mist no longer felt like mist—it felt like smoke.

Something had happened. Or was about to.

Devananda sat in stillness, as he always did. But the stillness no longer mirrored the world. Outside, everything was beginning to shake.

Then, as if drawn from the well of memory, the words returned— spoken long ago in India, beneath a neem tree, when he still believed renunciation meant retreat.

"The *gunas* are the fabric of the world," his teacher had said. "Not good and evil. Not gods and devils. Just *tamas, rajas, sattva*—in endless interplay."

He remembered how, as a young man, the idea had comforted him.

But now it did not comfort. Now it unveiled.

"The rise of madness is not a glitch in the system," his teacher had said. "It is the system. *Tamas* must rise. *Rajas* must stir. *Sattva* must hold. If one is suppressed, the others erupt."

"Even violence?" Devananda had asked.

"Especially violence," his teacher replied. "It is part of the dream's rhythm. It comes when the dream forgets itself."

A knock broke the memory.

A boy this time. Wide-eyed. Breathless.

"They took Herr Braun," he said. "Just now. From the bakery."

Devananda's face didn't move, but something behind it did.

"Did anyone speak?" he asked.

The boy shook his head. "Everyone watched. No one spoke."

He nodded. The boy ran off.

Later, seated beneath the bare tree near his hut, Devananda felt the wind shift.

"This is not evil," he said aloud, not to excuse it, but to see it.

"This is *tamas*, rising because the world fed it. This is *rajas*, ignited by fear and hunger. This is the dream turning against itself— because it does not know it's dreaming."

"And we—we call it evil, because we are still asleep inside it."

His eyes closed. The breath slowed. The flame inside held steady.

"To see the *gunas* is not to escape them. It is to know their dance. And to no longer take their madness personally."

"The storm is not against me. It is simply a storm."

In that moment, a sound rose from the village below—shouting, boots, a door slammed open.

Devananda did not rise.

He bowed his head—not in fear, not in defiance, but in deep surrender.

"Let it play," he whispered.

"Let the dream exhaust itself."

What Remains

The fire did not come for him.

Not that week. Not the next. The world burned in its own way— names vanished from shop windows, boots echoed in the streets, and eyes learned not to look too long.

But no one came for the man in the hills.

They feared him. Or forgot him. Or perhaps the storm simply passed over, unwilling to disturb something that no longer resisted.

Devananda began to walk again.

Not far. Just to the edge of the trees, where smoke sometimes curled from chimneys that had gone cold, or where mothers whispered bedtime stories with new, tightened endings.

He spoke to no one, but he listened.

He did not teach, but he watched.

He did not interfere, but once, he left a bundle of herbs at a window, unseen.

The girl returned once, months later. Her mother had died. Her father was gone. She came not to speak, but just to sit by his fire.

They did not speak of doctrine. They did not speak of suffering.

Only once, as she looked at the flame, did she ask, "Will it end?"

He answered without turning.

"Everything ends. Except what watches."

One night, alone again, he sat by the fire and saw it flicker.

It hadn't gone out. Just flickered.

He felt no dread, no sadness.

"Maya doesn't end with knowledge," he thought. "It just stops fooling you."

The world still trembled. People still vanished. The wind still carried smoke.

But the silence inside him was different now. Not the silence of retreat, but of one who has passed through illusion and emerged still.

A Glass of Water

Prologue

The stage was already lit when I arrived.

A warm amber glow across a floor swept clean. A few props were scattered—an overturned stool, a brass pot, a wooden wheel. Nothing in its place yet. The back curtain rippled as if someone had just stepped offstage.

Lord Vishnu sat in the front row, legs crossed, a script in his lap.

He didn't look up as I approached. Just flipped a page and nodded to himself.

"Have we done this one before?" I asked.

He shrugged. "Does it matter?"

I took my place near the wings, adjusting my robes. The hem caught on a nail. I pulled it free without tearing. Somewhere overhead, someone adjusted a light. It hummed once, then held.

Vishnu stood and walked to the edge of the stage. He carried a small bell. It wasn't necessary, but he liked the sound it made.

"We'll take it from the top," he said. "You're center left. You cross to the river."

I waited for the cue.

He rang the bell—once, lightly. A single chime.

Then he looked at me and smiled, as if remembering something halfway between amusement and affection.

"A glass of water would be nice," he said absently, turning back to his script.

I nodded.

And I stepped forward.

The light shifted.
The set changed.
And the world began.

The River

The brass cup felt warm in my hand.

I had been walking a while. The sun was high, the sky blank and unconcerned. My feet kicked up dust that didn't rise far—just swirled around my ankles before falling again, tired like everything else.

It was Vishnu's request, of course. He had asked for a glass of water.

No thunder. No commandment. Just a quiet request beneath the neem tree, scratching the back of his neck and squinting at the heat shimmering off the road.

"Would you fetch me a glass of water?" he said—like a man asking for a second helping of lentils.

So I went.

The river was just beyond the tamarind grove. I had passed it before, I thought. Or maybe I had only heard of it. The trees rustled as I stepped through them, as if they'd been expecting someone but weren't sure it was me.

At the bend in the river, I saw her.

She was crouched at the bank, drawing water into a brass pot. Her sari clung to her ankles. Her bangles made music as she moved. A strand of hair slipped across her cheek, and she brushed it away without thought.

And just like that, I forgot the taste of the sky.

I didn't speak. I only watched.

She turned—perhaps sensing me—and smiled. Not a smile meant to enchant. Just the kind villagers give to strangers when the day is too beautiful to hold back warmth.

But something in me shifted. A small, strange tug. As if a thread, long buried, had been pulled.

"Are you lost?" she asked.

"No," I said—though I wasn't sure.

She tilted her head, studying me. "You look as if you've never seen a river before."

"I haven't," I said.

She laughed. It was a clear sound—nothing mystical or alluring. But it echoed in my chest as though it had been waiting there.

I asked her name. She gave it. I forgot the sound as soon as she spoke it—only remembering the way her lips shaped it.

She picked up her pot and turned toward the trees.

"Wait," I said, though I had no question.

She paused.

"I'm… looking for water."

She raised an eyebrow, amused. "Then you've come to the right place."

And she walked away—not like someone inviting me to follow, but like someone certain I would.

I looked down at the cup in my hand.

Empty.

Again.

Somewhere, very far away, someone was waiting for a glass of water.

But here, in this quiet place between water and wind, it seemed he could wait a little longer.

A Little While Longer

I did not follow her right away.

Instead, I sat beside the river, letting my fingers comb through the current like it was hair I once knew. The water was cool, thin, and alive. I cupped a handful and let it pour back through my palms, listening to how it did not answer me.

The sun had begun its descent. Its light stretched long across the trees, turning every leaf gold on one side and black on the other. Shadows moved without sound. A frog leapt from a rock into the shallows and vanished without a trace.

The wind carried the scent of tamarind, wet clay, and something sweet I couldn't name.

I told myself it was good to rest. Even the gods pause between acts of creation. What harm in a moment? I had been sent to fetch water, after all. And hadn't I found it? In the same way a singer finds a silence, or a pilgrim finds a place they don't mean to stay—but do.

She had been kind. That was all. A girl at the river. A smile in sunlight. No enchantments. No illusions. Just a presence that made the air seem easier to breathe.

Surely the Lord would not begrudge me a few hours here. After all, the world itself was His design—was it not wise to admire the craftsmanship? Study the structure? Learn the flavors of its breath?

I reached for my vina, intending to strum a few notes to mark the moment.

It wasn't there.

Strange.

I never travel without it.

I patted my side, then the small pouch across my chest. Gone.

Not lost—just… absent.

It struck me then—not as a warning, but as a curiosity. Like realizing you've forgotten a word, or a face you once loved, and it no longer feels urgent to remember.

No matter.

I lay back on the riverbank, my head resting in a cradle of warm grass. The earth beneath me was solid, generous, unhurried. A flock of parakeets passed overhead like a laugh with wings. I closed my eyes.

Her face rose again in the dark behind my lids—not radiant, not divine. Just… real. The way her eyes had met mine without hesitation. The round wet mark the pot had left against her hip. The loose hair that did not care who saw it.

I opened my eyes.

A few hours, then. Perhaps a day. I could learn her name again. Ask what the villagers called this river. Learn how they boiled their rice. Ask which god they whispered to before sleep.

To know the world is to know its Maker more fully. Isn't that what I have always done?

I stood slowly. Brushed the grass from my robes. My legs felt a little heavier than before, but not unwilling.

Just for a little while longer.

The Village

The path she had taken wound gently between trees, past a rusted ox-cart half-swallowed by vines. I followed without meaning to follow—my feet moved as if they had once known the way and only needed reminding.

Soon the trees thinned. The air grew warm and dense with the smell of smoke, turmeric, and cow dung. I heard voices—low and practical, punctuated with laughter. And then I saw them.

Thatched roofs like crouching animals. Whitewashed walls cracked with heat. A courtyard where chilies dried on a mat and a baby toddled between hens. A boy chased a goat with a stick, yelling something about a mango thief.

She was there, walking ahead of me, her pot balanced on her hip now like a sleeping child.

No one looked at me strangely. No one asked where I had come from.

Strangers arrive sometimes, the elders would later say. Especially during festival season. Must be here for the rites. I nodded when they told me this, and said nothing more.

Her name, I learned, was Meera.

She lived with her father, a potter whose fingers were always grey with clay and who walked with a limp that turned each step into a question. His voice was dry and slow, like wood being carved. He studied me for a long time before offering a place to sleep—under the awning behind his kiln.

In exchange, I could help him fire the pots.

I accepted.

It was good to work with my hands again.

There was a kind of listening in shaping clay. It taught you things: where to press, where to wait, when to let go. The fire, too, was its own teacher—impatient, greedy, easily offended. I liked the way it roared in the early morning, when the air was still cool and the sky looked bruised.

Meera brought us meals—flatbread wrapped in banana leaves, lentils spiced with mustard seed. She never stayed long, but her presence remained after she left, like the smell of warm stones after rain. Once, she laughed at something her father said, and the sound passed through me like a breeze through tall grass—nothing touched, yet everything moved.

The days unfolded gently. Not with urgency, but with rhythm.

Children ran barefoot through the alleys, shrieking with joy or hunger. Women gathered to pound grain, their songs rising and falling in loose harmony. A monkey stole an oil lamp from the temple and was chased across three rooftops before it dropped it into a basket of onions. The priest declared it a bad omen; the village women declared it a good story.

In the evenings, we sat around a central fire.

The elders smoked thin pipes that smelled of fennel and damp bark. They told stories—not grand myths, but things that happened last year or last generation, depending on who was listening. One woman spoke of a snake that had lived in her grain jar for thirteen days without touching a single kernel. Another swore her dead husband had returned as a squirrel that only stole from her neighbor's tree.

I listened. I asked questions. I laughed at the right times.

I wasn't trying to become one of them.

But I was no longer entirely outside them, either.

At night, I lay on a mat beneath a torn mosquito net, the warmth of the kiln seeping through the wall behind me. I could hear the soft chime of Meera's bangles as she washed dishes. I could smell the river in the distance, quiet and unbothered by all our lives.

And each night, as my eyes closed, it seemed less and less strange that I had stayed.

The Days That Follow

The days lengthened—not in time, but in texture.
Mornings began with the rooster's complaints and the sharp scent of boiled guava leaves. Smoke rose from every roof like incense offered to no one in particular. A thin woman with three teeth sold fried lentil cakes wrapped in newspaper. I bought one each morning. She always gave me two.

The village unfolded itself to me, not all at once, but like a flower suspicious of too much light. Each day revealed a new detail—a shortcut through the tamarind grove, a boy who could mimic birdcalls so well he confused the real ones, a man who hadn't spoken since his wife died but still hummed lullabies.

I began to rise with the roosters—not from habit, but eagerness.

There was always something to do.

When the temple priest fell ill, I offered to recite the daily verses. No one asked how I knew them. The villagers said I had a memory like an elephant and a voice like a story someone had almost forgotten. I took it as a compliment.

When the river swelled one night and crept close to the grain stores, I joined the men who lined the banks with stones and old cloth. My hands blistered. I didn't mind. It felt good to be useful in ways that didn't require divinity.

One afternoon, a small girl named Rani went missing. Panic spread like smoke. Her mother wailed into the well as if her voice could reach the bottom. I found Rani asleep beneath a fig tree, clutching a broken doll.

I carried her back. The doll fell once and cracked open. Inside was a kernel of rice and a dead bee.

No one could explain it. The priest declared it a good omen.

That night, her mother left a bowl of milk and hibiscus petals at my door. Meera added a slice of jaggery.

Meera.

She had changed—or maybe I had learned how to see her. There was strength beneath her quiet. When she laughed, it was never to please. She knew how to read clouds and cows and children. Once, she warned her father not to fire a certain batch of clay pots. "They've been listening wrong," she said. He ignored her. The pots cracked.

She never said, "I told you so." She only looked at him as if she had already forgiven him for what hadn't yet happened.

We rarely spoke at length, but she sat beside me at the fire some evenings. Our arms would brush, and neither of us pulled away. Once, I handed her a carved mango pit I'd shaped during a long afternoon. She turned it over in her hand without a word, then slipped it into her sash.

There was a peace between us that didn't ask for names.

The village began to treat me differently. Children brought me flowers stolen from other shrines. A man with a boil on his back asked if I could pray it away. An old woman asked me to name her grandson.

One evening, two brothers were arguing over where to place a fence—each claiming the land was theirs. I stepped in—not with force, but with silence. I asked them how long they expected the earth to remember their names

They laughed, then sighed, then walked away.

Afterward, an elder pulled me aside and said, "You could be something more."

I didn't know what he meant.

But I liked the way he said it.

That night, beneath the mosquito net, with the kiln's warmth on one side and Meera's footsteps fading on the other, I stared into the dark and tried to recall a time before the village.

Nothing came.

Only the soft clink of bangles.

Only the breath of the river.

Only the feeling of being where I was supposed to be.

Firelight

There was a night when the fire burned low, and no one stirred it.

The others had gone—the elders to their huts, the children carried off half-asleep, even the dogs curled into themselves like punctuation marks. Only the coals remained, glowing softly beneath a hush that had thickened like milk left too long in the pot.

Meera and I were the last by the fire.

She sat across from me, cross-legged, her arms looped around her knees. Her bangles rested quietly on her forearms. Her hair was unbraided, and a single strand clung to the curve of her neck.

Neither of us spoke.

The silence between us wasn't empty. It had shape, weight. It pulsed gently, like something alive.

She picked up a stick and poked at the embers. Sparks rose, floated briefly, then died.

"I used to think fireflies were stars that forgot how to stay up," she said.

I smiled. "And now?"

"Now I think stars are fireflies that remember."

Her voice was soft, almost sleepy. She wasn't trying to be poetic.

She was just saying what came.

I watched her fingers, darkened at the tips with husk ash. Her nails were short, practical. She wore no ring. No thread around her neck. Just the moonlight on her skin and the scent of tamarind in her hair.

I reached for a twig and traced a circle in the dirt. She watched me.

"Sometimes," she said, "you look like you've forgotten something important."

"Do I?" I asked.

She nodded.

"But you also look like you're not in a hurry to remember."

That made me laugh—a quiet, startled sound that felt truer than anything I'd said all day.

The circle I was drawing broke. My hand stilled.

She reached over and smoothed the dirt with her palm. Slowly. Deliberately.

"I don't mind," she added. "Whatever it was."

The embers hissed as the wind shifted.

And for a moment, I forgot that I had ever forgotten anything at all.

The Festival of Lights

The festival of lights came early that year.

The rains had been generous. The rice grew tall and bowed at the waist, like people praying. The sun returned without malice—warm and golden, as if it too had been washed clean.

In the weeks leading up to the celebration, the village moved with a kind of music. Children strung marigolds into crooked garlands. Women painted their thresholds with rice paste and ash, drawing geometric blessings that looked like traps for gods. Even the potter—Meera's father—set aside his limp and began firing new lamps with the care of a man making something that might last beyond him.

They asked me to lead the chant that would open the festival.

I said yes without thinking.

I no longer thought of myself as someone who had once said no.

When the night came, the whole village gathered in the temple courtyard. Clay lamps were lit one by one, until the walls seemed to glow from within. Smoke curled up from incense bowls. The air was thick with the smell of ghee, sandalwood, and fried sweets.

I stood beside the priest, reciting verses I hadn't realized I still knew.

And then I saw her.

Meera stood among the women, holding a small lamp in both hands. Its flame flickered against her face, caught in her lashes, made her eyes burn gold. Her hair was half-loose, curled from the humidity. Her bangles caught the firelight with every breath.

She wasn't looking at me.

But she knew I was looking at her.

After the prayers and sweets and dancing—after the children fell asleep in piles and the music faded into soft humming—she found me.

We sat behind her father's house, near the embers of the cooking fire. A half-eaten sweet rested on a banana leaf between us. Smoke drifted through the banyan leaves above.

"I liked your singing," she said.

I shrugged. "The tune is older than anything."

She smiled. "That's true of most things worth hearing."

We sat like that for a long time—no rush, no reason to move. The fire cracked softly. Somewhere in the dark, someone was telling a story to a half-listening dog.

"Why did you stay?" she asked—not accusing, not even curious. Just tracing the shape of a thought.

I opened my mouth, but nothing came.

I could not remember arriving.

Only being.

"I suppose," I said, "this is where I belong."

She looked at me—not with surprise, but something quieter. Like recognition.

"Maybe," she said. "Maybe you always did."

The Wedding

The morning of our wedding, the neem tree bloomed.

It hadn't flowered in years. The potter said it was too old. Meera said it was too tired. But that morning, without wind or warning, it burst into blossom—white buds clinging to every branch like the tree had remembered something just in time.

The priest called it a sign. The potter said we should hurry before the rains came.

No one asked what I thought.

I had no thoughts—only the low hum behind my ribs that returned whenever Meera's eyes found mine and didn't look away.

We were married beneath the neem tree at dusk. The women strung garlands from its branches, some fresh, some already wilting. A girl too young to speak carried a bowl of rosewater and poured it along the path, leaving a glistening trail between worlds.

The village gathered. There were no invitations—just food and fire, and people arriving in the clothes they had. Someone played a drum. Someone else joined with a reed flute that couldn't hold a tune but tried anyway.

Meera wore red—not the quiet red of ceremony, but the kind that looked like it had grown from her own skin. A line of turmeric traced her collarbone, and jasmine in her hair kept slipping free.

She didn't smile. But her mouth held the memory of one.

We circled the fire seven times. On the last round, we walked together. The dust lifted gently beneath our feet. I don't remember the words the priest said. I remember her hand in mine—warm, dry, certain.

Someone shouted that the sky was crying.

And it was.

The first rain of the season came in soft pearls, falling slow and sparse—just enough to stir the scent of earth without soaking our clothes. The crowd clapped. The priest raised his hands. Meera turned her face upward, and when she looked at me again, her cheeks were streaked and shining.

Later, inside our hut, she sat cross-legged on the mat and removed her bangles one by one, placing them in a clay bowl beside the door.

That bowl would later fill with ashes, milk, loose buttons, and the bones of rats we didn't want to kill but couldn't let live.

She leaned forward, touched my face with her thumb, and said, "Now you have no excuse not to stay."

"I never wanted one," I said.

She laughed—low, tired, real.

And when we pressed together beneath the mosquito net, our bodies slick with sweat and dust and rice flour from the day's celebration, I forgot everything that came before her mouth.

Outside, the frogs began singing.
A rhythm older than language.
A rhythm of first nights.
Of things that didn't need to be spoken aloud.

The Days After

In the first days after the wedding, time softened.

Mornings came late. We woke with the light, not the roosters, and only rose when the warmth made the mosquito net unbearable. Sometimes we didn't speak. Sometimes we did—about nothing: the shape of a cloud, the bitterness of tamarind, whether the dog that barked every night had a wife.

Meera laughed more now, but never loudly. Her laughter was like the cloth she washed by the river—worn, clean, still strong.

She took over the cooking. I offered to help, but she refused.

"You've already done enough," she said. "You married me."

I made myself useful where I could. Repaired the roof with palm thatch. Mended a fence the goats kept testing. Dug a trench to divert the rainwater that pooled in the corner of our hut. Once, I brought her a frog with markings like Sanskrit along its back.

She stared at it for a long time.

"Put it back," she said.

We went to the river in the afternoons, sometimes together, sometimes not. If I arrived first, I'd sit on the bank with my feet in the water, watching the current toy with leaves like children who didn't know they were being led. If she arrived first, she'd be rinsing vegetables or scrubbing pots, her hair tied up with whatever cloth she had nearest, a smear of ash on her cheek.

We didn't show much—not in front of others. But our hands

found each other often: passing a ladle, brushing shoulders in the doorway, sitting side by side in the fading heat. Once, when I handed her a cup of buttermilk during a village gathering, our fingers touched for just a moment too long. No one said anything.

At night, she slept curled toward me, her breath soft against my collarbone. I liked to listen to the rhythm of it—the pause she took just before exhaling, as if even in sleep, she was deciding whether to stay.

The village noticed, of course.

A woman at the well said Meera's skin had begun to glow. A boy asked me if I was a magician, because Meera had smiled at him and it made his stomach hurt.

Even her father softened. He didn't say much, but one evening he brought me a cup of toddy, handed it over without a word, and walked away chewing his betel like it owed him money.

Nothing grand happened.

Just hours, stitched into days, stitched into something we stopped counting.

It was a season of closeness—of held gazes and unheld time.

And though I did not know it then, these were the days I would return to later—when the river rose, and the sky cracked, and the glass I had been meant to fill shimmered again in my hand.

The First Cry

It began with silence.

Not the silence of night, or of two people resting back to back in the dark. This was different. A pause inside Meera that lasted three days longer than it should have. Her body, usually so precise—waking with the sun, bleeding with the moon—went quiet.

She said nothing at first.

But I noticed how she started turning in bed with more care. How she stopped sitting cross-legged and began sleeping with a cushion between her knees. How she touched her belly when she thought no one was watching.

On the fourth day, I asked what she was thinking.

She said, "I think something small has entered me."

I didn't understand, not then. I asked if it hurt.

She laughed. "Not yet."

She never said the word. Neither of us did. But we began moving differently. I carried heavier loads from the market. She stopped bathing alone in the river. When she cooked, she sat on a low stool instead of squatting near the fire.

The changes came slowly.

Her walk shifted—first subtly, then unmistakably—hips rocking slightly, as if the earth had begun to turn beneath her. Her hunger sharpened. She ate mangoes with chili, then wanted only milk. Some days she couldn't stand the smell of ghee. Other days, she cried while peeling onions and said it wasn't the onions.

Her belly grew.

At first, just a soft rounding. Then firmer. Heavier. The village women came and placed their hands on it like reading a warm stone. They smiled and nodded and said nothing useful.

I watched her body change with awe and a strange kind of grief. She was still Meera—but slower, deeper, more elemental. Like a mountain slowly remembering it was once fire.

She complained of backaches. Of dreams she couldn't explain. Once she said she felt the child kick, and grabbed my hand to place it on her stomach. I felt nothing—but I nodded.

In her eighth month, Meera began to insist that the child was eavesdropping.

"He hears what I think," she said.

I laughed, until one day she whispered, I want guava, and a ripe one dropped from the roof with a soft thud.

"It's just wind," I said.

She nodded. But the next day, when she muttered not ghee again under her breath, the entire tin spoiled.

After that, we fed her only what she pretended not to want.

We didn't count the months. No one did. We simply lived through them.

The rains came and went. The river rose, receded, left behind silt and silence. The kiln cooled. Her father moved more slowly. The village seemed to lean inward, as if bracing for something.

And then, one morning before dawn, she woke me with a sound I had never heard from her before.

Not fear. Not pain. Just—insistence.

It was time.

The women came quickly, as if summoned not by voice but by rhythm. They filled the hut with smoke, sweat, boiling water, and murmured prayers. I was sent outside. Given a bowl of turmeric paste to stir and told not to stop. So I didn't.

Hours passed.

Then: a cry.

High and fierce. Not the cry of a fragile thing, but of something newly claimed.

A woman emerged, her arms wet with blood and milk. She handed me the child, wrapped in cotton already stained.

A boy.

His eyes opened once—unfocused, searching for nothing. Then he sneezed.

That night, as Meera lay half-asleep with the baby curled against her, she whispered a name. I repeated it once, so softly I barely heard myself say it.

Then I lay beside them, my hand resting lightly on the edge of the mat, as if to keep them from drifting too far from me.

Just Before Dawn

Just before dawn, I heard a frog croaking near the kiln.

At first it sounded like nonsense—a wet, throaty baritone bubbling from the mud:

"A-vid… a-vid… a-vid…"

Then, suddenly—loud and sharp:

"Avidya!"

I froze.

The frog didn't move. It sat on a patch of brick, throat still pulsing, eyes fixed on nothing in particular.

By the time I stepped outside, it was gone.

I didn't tell Meera. What would I say?

That morning, the child took his first step.

Our son learned to walk in the space between monsoons.

One moment he was crawling, dust on his knees and mouth always wet with questions, and the next he was upright—arms outstretched, legs unsteady—shouting his triumph with every step, as if he had invented the act itself.

Meera watched him with quiet pride. She never praised loudly—just nodded, as if he had finally done what she'd always known he would. But later, when she thought I wasn't watching, I saw her bury her face in the corner of her sari and laugh until her shoulders shook.

We named him Aru.

Not after a god or a star or a family line, but after a sound he made as a baby when he tried to call the wind.

Aru was stubborn. He refused to eat if the food was too hot, refused to sleep unless he was between us—one hand on each of our chests, like a bridge. His hair grew in wild tufts. His voice carried through the trees.

He was ours. Utterly.

The days grew long and sticky. The air smelled of ripe guava and pressed earth. Meera tied her hair up every morning and let it fall again by noon. I worked in the kiln with the potter and showed Aru how to roll little beads of clay between his fingers.

Sometimes he'd press them into his mouth and declare them sweet.

He had favorite things—a bent spoon, a yellow string, the ghee tin with a dent in the side. He dragged them everywhere like small sacred relics. Once, he hid the temple bell under our sleeping mat. We found it only after three days of wondering if the gods had taken offense.

He was two when he first said my name.

Not "father," not "appa," not anything formal. Just my name—as if we were equals, co-conspirators in the game of living.

Meera heard it from across the courtyard and didn't say a word. But that night, she sang to him while feeding him lentils, and I swear her voice changed.

It carried something deeper.

Something I hadn't heard since the night we first lay together, listening to frogs and stars.

The Clay Jar

One afternoon, the potter called me to the kiln—not with words, but with the sound of his limp.

Soft, regular.

He held a cracked jar in his hands.

"Fix it," he said.

I took the jar, turned it slowly. The break was clean—a fault along the base, as if it had snapped from its own weight.

"I could patch it," I said. "But it won't hold water."

He grunted. "Then make something new."

He handed me a lump of fresh clay, already damp, already waiting.

We worked in silence.

The kiln hissed in its low, hungry way. Aru was nearby, asleep in the shade with one of Meera's scarves draped over his stomach. Meera was at the well with the other women, her voice occasionally floating above the splash of water and gossip.

The potter's hands were slower now. His limp more pronounced. But his fingers still knew the shape of a pot before it was born. He pressed the wheel pedal with the edge of his good foot and said, without looking up, "The boy's growing."

"He is."

"Too fast."

I didn't answer. He was right.

"He looks like you," he added.

I smiled. "That's his only flaw."

The potter laughed—once, short and dry. "Don't let your love soften your hands."

He stopped the wheel. Lifted the clay off gently.

"Fire makes everything true," he said.

"A crack before the kiln is a mercy.

A crack after means you've lied to yourself."

He handed me my half-shaped jar.

It was crooked. But I couldn't tell if it was the clay or my hands that had faltered.

Later that evening, I found him asleep in his chair with Aru curled in his lap, both of them breathing in the same rhythm. The half-finished jar sat nearby, drying in the late light.

That night, Meera placed it by the door.

"Don't fix it yet," she said.

"Why not?"

She looked at it. At me.

"Let it harden.

Let it tell you what kind of thing it is."

The Boat

It was Meera who mentioned him first.

We were eating mango slices on the veranda, Aru asleep with his mouth open, one hand still clenched around a piece of string. The sun was low, dragging long gold across the courtyard. The flies had grown bold.

"There's a man building a boat," she said, absently.

I looked up. "In the river?"

She shook her head. "In his house."

I laughed. "Is he mad?"

She shrugged. "He's old."

That was the end of it—or so I thought.

A few days later, I passed his hut on my way to the kiln. The door was open. Inside, the floor had been cleared of furniture. A frame of thick wooden ribs curved from wall to wall like the skeleton of something waiting to be remembered.

He was sanding one of the planks with slow, methodical care. His hands moved like they were tracing something already finished.

I stood in the doorway for a while.

He didn't greet me. Didn't pause. Just looked up once and said,

"Water comes where it is owed."

Then he returned to his work.

Later, I asked Govind, the oldest man in the village, about him.

"That's Hari," he said, chewing betel. "Widowed. Doesn't speak much since the fever took his daughters. Used to be a fisherman, before the river swallowed his nets."

"Has he done this before?"

"Built a boat?"

"No. Waited for something that isn't coming."

Govind spat into the dust. "Everyone here does that."

A few children began hanging around his hut, whispering theories. Some said he'd had a vision. Others said he was building it for the gods. One girl swore she saw him talking to birds.

Aru asked me if we could visit. I told him no.

"He's not building it for us," I said.

Aru thought about this for a moment, then nodded solemnly— the way children do when they're not sure they understand, but feel they should pretend they do.

After that, we all went on pretending.

We fetched water. We told stories. We folded clothes.

And in the center of a dry village,

a boat grew.

The Search

Aru disappeared on the second day of the rains.

It began like any other monsoon morning: the smell of wet soil, the frogs calling from hidden places, water threading down the thatch roof in silver ribbons. Meera had tied her hair up in a scarf and was kneading dough when she noticed the silence.

"Where's Aru?" she asked.

I looked toward the corner where he usually played with his bits of string and clay beads. The bowl was overturned. The mat was empty.

"He was just here," I said, standing.

We searched the hut first. Then the courtyard. Then the neighboring houses.

Nothing.

By the time the potter joined us, limping through puddles with his hands shaking, the village had already begun to murmur.

Meera's face had gone cold. Still. She didn't cry. She didn't speak. She simply moved—from house to house, calling his name, her voice growing smaller each time.

"Aru," I shouted, pacing in widening circles.

No answer.

A woman near the well said she'd seen him walking toward the trees. Another said she saw him near the canal. A third swore she saw him talking to Hari—the old man with the boat.

I ran there. Burst into his hut without asking.

The boat had grown larger. It filled the space like a sleeping beast. Hari stood beside it, hammer in hand.

"I'm looking for my son," I said.

He didn't answer. Just stared at me, eyes steady.

"Did he come here?"

"Not for me," Hari said. "Not yet."

I left without another word.

The rain fell harder. It was past noon.

Govind organized a search. Men scattered into the fields, the riverbanks, the trees. Meera refused to stay home. Her scarf soaked through. Her feet slipped in the mud.

By evening, people were lighting lamps—not for prayer, but for light, as if the darkness might give something back.

Then, just before nightfall, someone shouted from the far end of the canal.

We ran.

He was there.

Aru.

Sitting in the curve of a washed-out gully, shivering, covered in mud and mosquito bites. His hands clutched a little raft of sticks and string, half-crumbled from the rain.

Meera dropped to her knees. Pulled him to her chest. Said his name three times, then fainted.

I carried them both home.

That night, he said nothing. Just lay between us, awake, staring at the roof, his small hands opening and closing.

When he finally spoke, his voice was barely a whisper.

"I was waiting," he said.

"For what?" I asked.

He didn't answer.

The Years That Followed

Years passed like weather—noticeable only when they changed.

Aru grew tall. His voice deepened. His hair curled more tightly when it rained. He no longer slept between us but now on a mat of his own, where he would lie for hours staring at the ceiling, lips moving silently as if reciting conversations from dreams.

He had taken to making kites—delicate, spined with bamboo and stitched from old sari scraps. Some were shaped like birds, others like eyes. He'd let them loose on windless days, claiming the sky just needed coaxing. When one finally rose, he'd whisper something to it, then let the string slip from his fingers.

The potter's limp worsened. He taught fewer apprentices but made more cups—tiny ones, the kind no one used but everyone admired.

"If the gods ever return," he said once, "they'll want tea."

Meera began to hum when she worked. Always the same tune. Wordless, lilting—a song she'd never admit to knowing.

Our lives had shape now.

Aru fetched water from the well. I worked with the grain merchants during the dry months and the ferrymen during the rains. Meera became the quiet center of everything—called to births, to funerals, to disputes about boundary stones.

No one asked if I was from here anymore.

I was.

There were good days—harvests that came early, festivals with extra oil for lamps, and a rooster that would follow the temple priest everywhere, as if awaiting instruction.

And there were bad ones—a stomach sickness that passed through the village like smoke, a fire that claimed three huts and nearly a fourth. Once, a baby was born with no cry. Meera held it longer than anyone else, as if her silence could teach it how.

Through it all, time thickened. Our steps slowed. The river

changed course slightly one year, and everyone pretended not to notice.

We spoke of building a new room for Aru.

Of planting neem instead of tamarind.

Of buying a second goat.

The days were not remarkable.

But they were ours.

And somewhere at the edge of all this—quietly, steadily—

a boat waited in the shadows of a hut.

Still unfinished.

Still growing.

Clay and Fire

The day the potter handed me his tools, it wasn't a ceremony.

He didn't say he was done. He didn't call it a gift.

He simply set his hands on the wheel and said,

"Your turn."

Then he walked away.

By then, his fingers had grown stiff. His eyes had begun to miss the details. The last pot he'd fired was lopsided, the base too thin. But he'd laughed when it cracked and said it was just proving it had character.

I began slowly.

Fixing his old kiln. Cleaning the shed. Sorting through shelves of discarded glazes and forgotten molds.

Meera helped. She kept the books, bartered for clay, argued with the men who delivered it, and never once let them charge more than they had the week before.

Aru carved small patterns into the pots—birds, leaves, strange creatures he refused to name.

We became known for them.

People came from other villages to buy them. They said the patterns changed when you turned them in the light.

We hired two apprentices. Built a second wheel. Fired the kiln twice a week, sometimes three.

The clay was good that year—red and heavy.

It made deep-sounding pots, the kind that held silence even when empty.

I found myself waking before dawn. Wanting to feel the weight of the earth between my hands. Wanting to shape something that might last longer than I would.

Once, while trimming a vase, I caught Meera watching me from the doorway.

"You've become him," she said.

"Who?"

She nodded toward her father, asleep in the shade with his legs tucked up like a child's.

"The man who taught you the wheel."

I looked at my hands. They were calloused. Burned.

Stained with red dust that wouldn't wash out.

She was right.

But I didn't say so.

The Quiet Years

There came a time when the village forgot what it used to be.

The tamarind trees at the southern edge were cleared to make space for more houses. New families arrived—relatives of relatives, strangers with familiar names. The temple courtyard was expanded.

A second well was dug.

One man opened a sweets stall. Another began selling thread.

Someone built a roof tall enough to see the river bend in both directions.

People started using the word before more often.

"Before the new houses."

"Before the fire."

"Before Aru was walking."

Even I said it, without thinking.

The clay changed, too. A little softer. More silt. It required longer drying.

I adjusted without complaint.

The wheel felt natural in my hands now, like it had been passed through generations I had forgotten I belonged to.

Meera grew quieter in those years.

Not withdrawn—just still.

She had always worked efficiently, but now there was grace to it. A kind of knowing. She would sweep the courtyard before sunrise, and I'd catch her standing in the dawn light, eyes closed, face tilted upward like a seed waiting for rain.

Aru grew into his limbs. His voice deepened. His hair never settled.

He began carving small figurines—animals, gods, shapes he never named.

Some he buried in the garden.

Others he lined along the windowsill, as if waiting for them to wake.

The village spoke of turning the canal into a full irrigation channel.

The men argued about where to divert the water.

Meetings were held.

Nothing changed.

A traveling merchant came one summer with stories of a war beyond the hills.

No one listened.

A woman gave birth to twins with hair already braided.

The priest declared it auspicious.

Time passed like wind through thick grass—seen only in how the light moved.

Sometimes I would pause at the kiln, hands coated in clay, and listen to the sounds of the village:

Pounding grain.

Laughing children.

Goats arguing with no one.

It felt… full.

Not happy. Not sad.

Just complete, in the way a bowl is complete once it holds something warm.

That was the morning he arrived.

A man with a crooked shawl and sandals made of rope. He walked with the easy rhythm of someone who didn't need to be anywhere. His beard was white. His eyes—too bright.

"Which way to the river?" he asked me, though it was plainly in sight.

I pointed.

He didn't move.

"You still have time," he said. "But not as much as you think."

Then he smiled. Not kindly. Not cruelly. Just… knowingly.

I opened my mouth to ask something, but he was already walking. His staff tapped softly on the path.

I told Meera later. She said, "Maybe it was a sadhu."

"Maybe," I replied. "He asked the way to a river he could see."

She shrugged. "Gods play tricks. So do fools."

We didn't talk about it again.

The Air Between Storms

The air turned first.

Not with wind or rain, but with something stranger—a pressure, as if the sky had leaned in too close to listen and forgot to pull away. The trees stopped rustling. The birds vanished. Even the insects seemed unsure, dragging their wings low and slow, like everything had grown too heavy to rise.

The villagers called it the thick time.

Old women covered their mirrors. Children were made to nap twice a day, though none could sleep. Everyone moved slower, as if each motion had to be paid for in sweat.

By the third day, shirts clung to our backs before dawn.

By the fifth, no one cooked indoors.

The thatch roofs felt like they might catch fire from the inside.

The river became a refuge. Not for bathing. For surviving.

Men stood waist-deep in the current, arms crossed like trees waiting for lightning.

Women sat in silence, legs trailing into the water, whispering instead of laughing.

Even the buffalo wandered in and refused to come out, eyes half-lidded in the muddy shallows.

Children floated on reed mats, speechless.

Meera and I joined them.

But Aru refused.

He had grown lean in the last year—shoulders broader, eyes sharper, voice thick with something he hadn't yet learned to name. He ate when he felt like it. Slept wherever sleep found him. Sometimes he vanished for hours and returned with nothing but silence.

That morning, he climbed to the roof and stayed there all day.

Shirtless.

Arms folded.

His skin glistened with sweat and sunlight.

He watched us below like characters in a story he'd already outgrown.

Meera shaded her eyes and looked up at him.

"He's sulking," she said.

But her voice carried something else—

Not worry.

Not yet.

But a premonition.

That evening, I walked home alone.

The path silent but for the soft squelch of my own steps.

The sky overhead was the color of boiled iron—not stormy, just full.

Taut.

Like the drum skin before the first beat.

I passed Hari's hut.

The door was open.

Inside, the boat stood finished.

It filled the space entirely—no room for a chair, or a mat, or a life.

It gleamed with oil and resin.

A thick coil of rope lay wound like a snake beside it.

The hull was dark, smooth, perfect.

Hari stood at the bow, polishing a brass bell with the sleeve of his shirt.

He looked at it like someone remembering a name not spoken in years.

He didn't look at me.

I didn't speak.

At home, Meera sat with a bowl of chopped vegetables she hadn't touched.

The knife lay beside her on the mat.

Her eyes were on the sky.

"Aru?" I asked.

She pointed toward the canal.

I found him standing at the edge of the water. Not in it—just at it.

Still.

He didn't look up when I approached.

"What are you doing?" I asked.

"Watching," he said.

"For what?"

He didn't answer.

Just turned and walked away.

That night, he went to bed early.

Meera didn't speak.

I didn't ask.

And outside, the air held its breath a little longer than it should have.

The Dream

It was just before dawn when I felt her shift beside me.

Meera rarely moved in her sleep. She slept like someone making peace with gravity—deep, still, surrendered. But that morning, she stirred. Turned away. Then back. Her breath caught, once.

When she woke, the light was only beginning to sift through the thatch—thin and pale, the color of smoke before it remembers fire.

She sat up slowly, her hand resting on her belly, though there was nothing there now to carry.

I waited.

Sometimes she spoke without prompting.

Sometimes she didn't.

This time, she did.

"I dreamed of crows," she said.

I rubbed my eyes. "They're always around."

"No," she said, quietly. "Not like this. They weren't moving. Just… standing. All of them. Lining the river. Hundreds. Facing the water."

Her voice wasn't shaken. Just thoughtful. As if trying to remember something that hadn't yet happened.

"And then," she added, "they stepped in. One by one. No flapping. No sound. Just… gone."

I sat up beside her. "Was it the storm dream again?"

"No," she said. "This one was quiet."

She stood, brushed her hands on her sari, and went to light the stove. As if that were the end of it.

But all day she moved a little slower.

Missed a step while sorting grain.

Forgot the salt in the lentils.

Stood too long at the window while Aru carved patterns into a gourd he didn't plan to keep.

That evening, I asked if she'd told anyone else.

"No one wants a dream right now," she said.

And that night, when she lay beside me again, she reached for my hand—

something she hadn't done in a while.

Her palm was warm. Dry.

Still holding something.

That night, after she slept, I stepped outside to breathe. The rain had not yet returned, but the air felt heavy with its promise. I looked toward the river.

On the far bank, barely visible in the starlight, a single crow stood. Facing the water. Silent. Motionless.

Then it stepped forward. One foot. Then the next. Into the dark.

Gone.

The Festival

It was the Festival of First Light—the day each year when lamps were floated down the canal to honor the changing season and the river that made the village possible.

For as long as anyone could remember, it had been a celebration of certainty:

that rains would come and go,

that fields would rise and fall,

that gods would keep their part of the bargain—

so long as lamps were lit and songs were sung.

This year, the sky didn't look right.

It wasn't cloudy—not exactly.

It was smooth. Featureless.

Like the inside of a bowl.

Light came through it dimly,

as though the sun had forgotten its name.

Still, the preparations went on.

Children plucked marigolds from the temple wall.

Women twisted them into garlands with thread and hope.

The boys practiced drumming near the canal,

beating old rhythms with new arrogance.

Meera didn't braid her hair that day.

When I asked why, she said,

"There are better things to do when the wind holds still."

But no one else seemed to notice.

Or if they did, they pretended not to.

By sunset, the whole village had gathered—

some in their finest,

some barefoot,

all expectant.

Clay lamps were handed out, one by one.

A new boy had been chosen to lead the procession.

He trembled with pride.

The priest smeared ash across his brow

and whispered a blessing into his ear—

a blessing the wind carried away

before anyone could hear.

The crowd formed lines as if choreographed.

The women adjusted their saris in unison.

The men raised their lamps on cue.

It looked—briefly—like a scene rehearsed a hundred times.

The procession moved toward the canal,

a line of flickering flame and loose song.
Old women swayed.
Young girls giggled.
Men shouted across the rows,
joking about whose lamp would go the farthest,
whose would sink,
whose might win a wife.
The river shimmered.
The lamps were released, one by one, onto its back.
Dozens at first. Then hundreds.
They bobbed and turned,
forming temporary constellations in the murky black.
Then—a drop.
Small. Sharp.
It struck a drumhead
with the sound of a snapped thread.
The drummer paused.
Then another drop.
And another.
The rain thickened.
A man near the bank lifted his face to the sky and let out a great
cheer.
"It's blessing rain!" he called.
Others laughed,
relieved to have been given something to name.
"Blessing rain!" they echoed.
And then—they danced.
They stomped their feet into the mud,
flung water into the air like holy dust,
sang louder to outpace the thunder

that hadn't come yet.
The children screamed and spun in circles.
Two boys grabbed a half-filled sack
and dragged each other through the shallows.
The drummer began again,
water now running down his arms.
Someone slipped,
fell into the canal,
and came up spitting and grinning.
"It's the gods!" someone shouted. "They've come to dance with
us!"
And so—they danced harder.
Even as the rain thickened.
Even as the garlands collapsed into wet tangles.
Even as the flame of every lamp hissed out,
one by one,
until only the river
shone with the dull reflection of a dying sky.
Meera didn't move.
She stood at the edge of the trees,
arms crossed,
eyes on the water.
I approached. She didn't turn.
"Not yet," she said. "The river hasn't woken."
Aru stood nearby,
arms limp at his sides.
His lamp floated already down the canal.
He watched it until it disappeared.
Then turned,
and walked home—

alone.

And somewhere,

in a hut no one visited,

a brass bell hanging from a boat's bow gave a single chime—

though no wind had stirred it.

The Flood

That night, the rain did not stop.

It did not soften. It did not rest.

It fell like something old—like the gods had remembered a debt and meant to collect it all at once. The roof groaned under it. The clay walls wept. The ground, which had once welcomed every drop, now began to repel it—no more, no more.

We had seen rain before. Loud rain. Cold rain. Rains that lasted days and left the fields singing.

This was different.

This was heavier.

By the second hour, the water reached the courtyard. The lanterns flickered, shadows twitching like animals caught in a snare. We moved what we could—cloth, grain, tools—lifting them higher, wedging them on rafters, tying them with rope already beginning to fray.

Meera's hands worked fast. Too fast. Her breath came short. Her hair clung to her neck, soaked already, though the rain was still outside.

"Where's Aru?" I asked.

She pointed—he was dragging the low stool to the door, peering out with eyes that no longer belonged to a child.

"Get away from there," I said.

He didn't move.

Then—a scream.

Not ours.

From the house next door.

Something crashing.

A woman's voice calling her son's name.

Then another—closer—shouting, "The goats! The goats are gone!"

I opened the shutters.

The canal was gone.

Or rather, it was everywhere.

A wide, moving sheet of black water, pulling trees at the root, lifting walls, sweeping baskets, animals, mats—anything not nailed to the earth.

A cart floated past, upside down.

Then the first wave hit.

It didn't knock. It entered—low at first, through the back wall, like a thief.

Then fast.

Fierce.

Angry.

We screamed.

I pulled Aru to me. Meera grabbed the rice sack and slung it over her shoulder without thinking. The potter—bless him—tried to save the clay gods from the hearth. They fell. Broke. One rolled under the cot and was never seen again.

The second wave shattered the front door.

We ran.

The water came with us.

Outside, someone shouted, "To the neem tree! To the neem tree!"

Another voice—older, rasping: "It's too late!"

We climbed—stumbling, barefoot, soaked. The mud sucked at our feet like it meant to keep us. A board struck the side of the kiln and splintered. Pots tumbled into the water, bobbed once, then broke like they'd never been made.

Aru slipped.

I caught him.

Meera turned to help—then cried out. A plank had hit her leg. She limped, teeth gritted. Still ahead of me.

We reached the foot of the hill near the temple. That was the plan—always the temple. Highest ground. Strongest stone.

We passed a broken wall near the edge of the potter's yard. Something metal glinted beneath it.

A bent mask.

I picked it up without thinking. It was painted like a lion's face— one used in village dramas. Splintered. Damp. The strap broken.

I turned it over. Frowned.

Then dropped it and ran.

The third wave didn't come with water.

It came with noise.

A sound like the sky collapsing.

We turned.

The kiln exploded—fire meeting flood, the hiss louder than thunder.

The roof of the potter's shed lifted and twisted, spinning once in the air before slamming into the neighbor's house.

Screaming. Screaming.

Too many voices.

Some in prayer.

Some in nonsense.

Some already gurgling.

Meera reached the first stone step.

Then the ground beneath her shifted.

She gasped—tried to grab the tree trunk beside her—

but the bark was slick.

I shouted her name.

She looked back at me.

And she was gone.

No splash.

No cry.

Just… gone.

Swept sideways into the dark like a thread pulled from a garment that doesn't even notice it's unraveling.

I lunged after her—

but the water caught my legs.

I nearly dropped Aru.

He was screaming now—fists clenched in my hair, eyes wide with the terror of something too big to be real.

I held him to my chest and ran—limping, sliding, half-crawling.

I don't remember reaching the steps.

Only climbing.

Only the temple's stone beneath my knees.

Only Aru in my arms.

Only the weight of one name screaming in my head like it might bring her back.

Epilogue

I woke with the sun on my face.

No room. No walls. Just sky—soft, unassuming. The earth

stretched around me, vast and rinsed clean, as if nothing had ever lived here.

I sat up slowly.

My clothes were torn. My hands caked in mud. There was no kiln. No temple. No neem tree. No Aru. No Meera.

Only silence. And something missing I didn't know how to name.

I walked.

The path back wasn't marked, but my feet knew it. The wind had erased my steps, but the silence remembered. I moved without hunger, without purpose, without anything tugging at me from behind or ahead.

Then I heard it.

"Ah, Narada," said a voice. Cheerful. Familiar. "There you are. I've been looking for you."

I turned.

Lord Vishnu was stepping lightly across the ruins—smiling, unhurried, as if the broken walls and scattered bodies were just props from a forgotten play.

He looked me over—mud-streaked, shaking, still stunned.

"You look awful," he said kindly. "Rough scene, was it?"

I couldn't speak. My throat was thick with grief, with loss, with something deeper than either.

He strolled past me, pausing to study the husk of a roof beam jutting from the mud. Then he turned back with a mischievous glint in his eye.

"All that," he said, gesturing wide, "and still no glass of water?"

I stared at him.

He shrugged. "Oh well. Easy to forget, isn't it?"

He stepped closer, his voice softening.

"You're suffering," he said. "I see that."

I lowered my head. "They were real. I held them. I loved them. They—"

"They were beautiful," he said gently. "But they were never yours to keep."

I sank to my knees. "Why does it hurt so much?"

He crouched beside me.

"Where does this pain come from, Narada?" he asked. "You knew about Maya. You knew all the teachings. You could explain them better than most."

I shook my head.

"And yet," he continued, "as soon as you stepped into the world— just to fetch a glass of water—you fell under the spell."

He looked out over the wreckage with a kind of affection.

"Pleasure, pain, family, fear, joy, grief… You knew it was illusion. But you forgot."

He smiled—not unkindly, but with something deeper.

"That is the power of Maya. Not just to trick the ignorant—but to enchant even the wise."

I buried my face in my hands. "I forgot who I was."

He stood.

"That's why we do these little rehearsals," he said. "To remind you."

He extended a hand.

"Come. Let's try the scene again."

I hesitated.

Then looked down.

At my feet lay a brass cup.

Dusty. Empty. Unchanged.

THE LOST UPANISHADS

Māyājāla Upanishad
(The Net of Illusion)

I. The Inquiry

The disciple asked the Teacher:

"Master, what is this net that glitters in every hand,

that hums in every home,

that binds the eye and the ear,

yet cannot be touched?"

The Teacher replied:

"It is the Māyājāla—the Net of Illusion.

Woven of names without bodies,

forms without substance,

sounds without source,

it stretches without end.

The ignorant call it progress.

The wise call it hunger."

The Net is spun of attention.

Its cords are craving,

its knots are habit,

its loom is desire.

Day and night it weaves,

and the more it grows,

the emptier it feels.

"But Master, does it not connect us?

Does it not bring news from afar,

faces of friends,
visions of the stars?"

"Connection without presence is bondage.
Knowledge without wisdom is weight.
The Net offers likeness in place of nearness,
streams in place of rivers,
noise in place of silence.
He who drinks only from it
is never quenched."

II. The Hidden Keepers

Invisible hands tend the Net.
They scatter images as hunters scatter seed.
They seek not your freedom,
but your gaze, your hours, your breath.
Thus beings are caught, not by chains,
but by their own thirst.

III. The Way Beyond

Not by fleeing the Net,
for it covers the earth.
Not by smashing it,
for thought cannot shatter thought.
Only by knowing:
"I am not the woven.
I am not the weaving.
I am the Seer of the Net,
the witness of all cords."

IV. The Resolutions

That Seer is unseen,
yet by Him all is seen.
He illumines the screen and the sky alike.
He watches the play of images,
but is untouched by their rise and fall.
The foolish chase the shadows.
The wise return to the Light.

Closing Benediction

From the Net, lead us to the sky.
From the flickering, to the steady.
From the restless, to the still.
From death, to Immortality.

ॐ शान्तिः शान्तिः शान्तिः ॥

Ātmā-Bāzār Upanishad
(The Marketplace of Selves)

I. The Market Opens

There is a bazaar where selves are sold.

At dawn the stalls are raised; by noon the shouting begins.

Here one may purchase a smile, there a following,

here a brand, there an avatar.

All are polished, all are packaged.

The sellers cry: "Buy a self, buy a self!"

At one stall, the influencer sells faces.

At another, the politician sells promises.

At another, the guru-for-hire sells enlightenment by subscription.

At another, Wall Street sells futures that have no future.

All are busy. All are loud. All are empty.

The buyers arrive with carts of attention.

Some pay with coins, others with years, others with their children's hours.

Each goes home with a mask.

Each says: "Now I am complete."

But the mask itches, and cracks, and slips away.

Tomorrow they return, hungrier than before.

II. The Teacher's Voice

A voice was heard, though none knew from where:

"O fools, the self you sell was never yours.

The self you buy will never fit.

The market is endless,
but the buyer and the seller are the same.
What you trade is what you lose."

III. The Paradox

He who buys many selves has none.
He who sells his self is not free, but chained.
He who refuses the market keeps what cannot be sold.
That which is not for sale is the true Self,
hidden in the crowd, silent behind the stalls.

IV. The Resolution

The market roars, yet the Self is still.
The masks crack, yet the Seer remains.
He who turns inward leaves the bazaar empty-handed,
but richer than all.

Closing Benediction

From the market, lead us to the home.
From the masks, to the face.
From the false, to the true.
From death, to the Deathless.

ॐ शान्तिः शान्तिः शान्तिः ॥

Antarmukha Upanishad
(The Inward Turning)

I. The Question
Where shall I go?
The roads are many, the voices loud,
each promising freedom,
each binding the feet.

II. The Teacher
Go inward.
The road is one.
It is short, yet endless.
It is narrow, yet boundless.
Few walk it, yet it is open to all.

III. That Which Binds
Turn inward, it falls away.
Turn inward, the crowd dissolves.
Turn inward, the idols crack.
Turn inward, the king is dust.

IV. The Seeing
He who looks outward is lost in images.
He who looks inward sees the Seer.
The Seer sees without being seen.
He knows without knowing.
He is silence within sound,
stillness within motion,

light within shadow.

V. The Paradox
Seek, and you will not find.
Stop seeking, and it is here.
Turn the gaze inward,
and the inward turns outward.
The seeker vanishes,
but That remains.

VI. The Resolution
The outward is endless;
the inward is whole.
The outward is many;
the inward is one.
The outward dies;
the inward is deathless.

Closing Benediction
From the outward, lead us inward.
From the restless, to the still.
From the seen, to the Seer.
From death, to the Deathless.

ॐ शान्तिः शान्तिः शान्तिः ॥